Insomnia...?

"I'm not sleepy." She sat upright. *"We could play gin rummy. There's a deck of cards in the drawer of the bed table."*

Grant approached the bed slowly. His glance traveled down from her attractively-tousled hair, past her questioning eyes, to take in the lovely figure revealed by the sheer chiffon. Then, deliberately, he leaned over and turned off the lamp. "We are not playing gin rummy," he said.

The room was bathed solely in the moonlight filtering through the filmy curtains. "I'm going out to the living room to read a dull book for a half hour. I'm not sleepy either."

His hand tightened on the door knob. "Unless you really want to complicate this impossible situation, you'd better start counting sheep. That way you won't come up with any more thin-skulled ideas." He gave a last baleful look at her motionless figure. "Gin rummy! My God—that will be the day!"

BRIDAL AFFAIR

by
Glenna Finley

A SIGNET BOOK
NEW AMERICAN LIBRARY
TIMES MIRROR

To Marian

SIGNET TRADEMARK REG. U.S. PAT. OFF. AND FOREIGN COUNTRIES
REGISTERED TRADEMARK—MARCA REGISTRADA
HECHO EN CHICAGO, U.S.A.

SIGNET, SIGNET CLASSICS, MENTOR, PLUME AND MERIDIAN BOOKS
are published by The New American Library, Inc.,
1301 Avenue of the Americas, New York, New York 10019

FIRST PRINTING, MAY, 1972

9 10 11 12 13 14 15 16

PRINTED IN THE UNITED STATES OF AMERICA

There is a tide in the affairs of women, which, taken at the flood, leads— God knows where.

—Byron

Chapter ONE

It was four months since Jean Cameron had come to live on the rugged piece of Oregon beach called Sea Bend and as she stood overlooking the churning Pacific breakers one evening in early April, she felt she would wither away and perish if she had to spend another two months there.

Not that Toby Calhoun, president of the Sea Bend Development Corporation, would encourage her demise. There was no place for bodies on his long, untrammeled ocean beach. Neither was there a place for automobiles, unlicensed beach fires, nor overnight campers. Pedigreed dogs were preferred and pedigreed beachcombers as well.

Jean suspected that the corporation issued specific orders as to the kind of driftwood the waves should bring in and arranged that any hapless dead fish washed ashore were neatly back in the briny by the next tide.

Life in Sea Bend was orderly and impeccable. By comparison, a cloistered nunnery sounded positively riotous and infinitely appealing.

As Jean moved on down the path leading to the beach, she was thinking that even her appearance didn't do much to improve the tone of Sea Bend. Her pale blue jeans hadn't started as stretch pants but after many washings they had turned out that way. Yellow canvas shoes had long since succumbed to the stains of seaweed and salt water while her white crew-necked sweater merely provided warmth under a serviceable pale yellow poplin jacket. It was a comfortable outfit but a far cry from the editorial decrees of *Harper's Bazaar*. It was even, she decided with amusement, a little shabby for Sea Bend.

"Hi, Miss Cameron!"

Her paperboy's piercing call brought Jean's thoughts abruptly back to the present.

"Hi Rick." She climbed up to the edge of the road as he slid his bike to a dramatic stop beside her. "How are things?"

"Pretty good." The nine-year-old towhead took her question seriously. "I even got a new subscriber a couple of days ago. He lives in that cottage of Mr. Calhoun's beyond Wailing Rock. Some kind of an artist, I guess."

"I didn't think anybody ever stayed in that until summer."

"Most generally they don't—with the rain and all" —Rick spoke with the casual sureness of a long-time resident—"but I guess Mr. Stevenson was willing to put up with the potholes in the road."

"Don't those potholes make delivering papers pretty rugged?"

A grin lit up his freckled face. "Not at the price Mr. Stevenson's paying . . . and he paid in advance. Boy! I've got enough clear profit to buy Max's food for a month."

Jean smiled in response. "I thought your mom told you to find a new home for that pet of yours."

"She did—but it takes a little time to find the right owner for a four-foot iguana."

"I can imagine. How did you get Max in the first place?"

"A neighbor of ours brought him back from Mexico. When they moved away from Sea Bend, they let me have him. 'Course he's grown a lot since he's been

8

at our house and he makes my mom sort of nervous. She's always afraid that he's going to get out of his cage and that she'll step on him."

Jean nodded sympathetically. "I can see her point of view."

"That's why she thinks he'd be happier living some place else." He gave her a thoughtful look. "Did I ask if you . . ."

She interrupted hastily. "Yes, you did, but I don't plan to stay in Sea Bend much longer than two more months."

Rick was puzzled. "No kidding. From the way my dad talked, I thought you were going to live here always like the rest of us. He was telling my mom that Mr. Calhoun was making plans for the two of you."

"You can never tell about women, Rick. I imagine Mr. Calhoun was spoofing somebody. Want me to take my paper and save you a trip up to my mailbox?"

"No—that's okay. But thanks anyway, Miss Cameron." His grin flashed again. "I'm just glad you don't want front-door delivery. It would take me an extra five minutes if I had to wheel my bike up that steep driveway of yours." He polished a smudge on his chrome handlebar. "It's almost worth it though, to come whizzin' back down. Boy! You must feel like you live on top of a mountain."

"I do," she told him. "Every time I struggle back up from a walk on the beach." She glanced at her watch. "If I don't get going, I won't make it back before dark. Give my regards to Maximilian."

"I will. See you, Miss Cameron." He gave a cheerful wave and rode off on the loose gravel roadbed with an expert's nonchalance.

Two sea gulls banked overhead as she retraced her way to the grassy path which ended in steep wooden steps down to the beach at her property line. The insistent south wind tousled her shiny brown hair and turned the tip of her nose a delicate pink. It also blew open the yellow windbreaker and whistled through her sweater like a piece of cheesecloth. Jean shivered once and reached down to zip the jacket closed, think-

9

ing she should have worn heavier clothing. At midday, April wore ruffles of summer; in late afternoon it still donned winter's cloak.

Overhead, dark gray clouds scudded northward as still blacker clouds filled the sky behind them. For the moment, she thought of abandoning her beach walk and retreating to the snug warmth of her hilltop house. Then she shook her head and tugged the jacket down further over her hips deciding that a brisk jaunt was necessary therapy to sort out her chaotic thoughts. Rick's words about her staying in Sea Bend had upset her. It was definite confirmation that Toby felt his courting campaign was nearing a successful end.

Jean compressed her lips as she kicked irritably at a piece of bark lying in the middle of the path. She kicked at the wood again and it skittered satisfactorily off the track and down the steep hillside onto the beach below. Jean's expression became even more stony as she surveyed that sandy expanse in front of her.

There was no doubt in her mind that Toby's ardor originated when he heard that she had inherited eight acres of ocean frontage next to his real estate development.

Not that Toby Calhoun needed any more property or money. He had inherited enough of both from his father to keep him knee-deep in chorus girls for the rest of his life. He had also inherited the physique of a surfing champion, a reckless grin, and fair hair which was sun-streaked from his hours on golf courses. When he was at his most persuasive, it was a minor miracle that Jean didn't fall at his feet like the rest of the feminine population of Sea Bend and points south.

Although not one to ignore a passing miniskirt, Toby's first love was his beach property, but when Jean appeared on the scene to take over the beach acres she had inherited from her uncle, Toby happily discovered that he could finally combine the best of both worlds. He was delighted that the new land owner was an attractive young woman in her mid-twenties with

10

a creamy complexion and as neat a pair of legs as had ever graced the sand at Sea Bend. There was also a charming snub nose and a deep blue-eyed glance that left him occasionally stammering like a schoolboy. The fact that she was unimpressed by his bank balance merely added zest to the chase.

From that day on, Toby set about his goals with the persistence of a dog retrieving a buried bone. There were only two things in Mr. Calhoun's mind: he wanted Jean and he wanted her eight acres.

But there remained the niggling question in Jean's mind as to which goal really came first.

If Rick was right, Toby obviously thought his campaign was about over. And since Toby was basically a very nice man, Jean didn't look forward to telling him that a victory banquet wasn't in the scheme of things.

"Damn!" she said feelingly. "What I need is a good red herring. Like an attractive blonde real estate broker to divert Toby." Her lips twitched in amusement as her thoughts bounded on. As long as she was providing the blonde for Toby, she might as well conjure up someone tall, dark, and handsome for herself!

The popping noise of a chain saw motor sliced through the silence as she arrived at the top of the steep stairs. She peered down to see which of Sea Bend's residents was replenishing his wood supply and the sight of a battered dune buggy with a crouching figure nearby made her smile and hurry down the steps.

"Hi Ernie!" she called a few minutes later when the saw was momentarily shut off.

A stocky Indian looked up, startled, at her peremptory call and then grinned as he identified her. "Hi yourself. You scared me out of two years' growth."

"That doesn't bother me, but if anybody reports that car of yours on the beach, Mr. Ravenwing—they'll fine you out of two months' salary." She picked her way over the pile of driftwood at the high-tide mark.

"Make it three," he said easily, reaching in his flannel shirt pocket for a cigarette and offering her the

11

pack. "Bartending at the Inn on off-season isn't so hot. The tips are way down."

She waited until he had lit both cigarettes and then said, "In that case, it's a good thing for you that Mr. Calhoun isn't on the beach this afternoon."

The laughter lines around his eyes deepened. "Red man smarter than squaw thinks. Big Chief Calhoun was up at the Inn for lunch and I heard him talking about looking at some property up the coast."

"I should have known."

"So I thought—why should I struggle with a wheelbarrow when I could whip down here in the buggy and do it in half the time." He inhaled deeply on his cigarette. "Nobody else is going to give it a second thought."

Jean nodded, knowing that Ernie's dune buggy wanderings were a tacit secret among most of the residents. Since he supplied a good part of Sea Bend's fireplaces with cut driftwood, it was to everyone's advantage to keep mum on his lawbreaking.

"Besides . . . Mr. Calhoun's a good scout," Ernie added as he leaned against the fender of his car. "I wouldn't be surprised if he didn't talk about going up the beach deliberately this afternoon. He knows I bring the buggy down here but he has to enforce the corporation's rules and regulations. He really takes this place seriously."

"I know."

"From what I hear around town, that isn't the only thing he takes seriously." His wrinkled face screwed up with amusement. "When are you going to put him out of his misery, Jean?"

"How do you know that I wouldn't be doing just the opposite?"

"The way he talks, he's sure willing to take the risk."

"You should know better than to take Mr. Calhoun seriously. I'm just handy to take out to dinner."

"Mebbe . . . but he's never stuck so close to Sea Bend at this time of year before. He's usually down in Palm Springs on a golf course." His look was

12

thoughtful. " 'Course he's never had a chance of getting your land before either."

"He hasn't now," she told him flatly. "I don't plan to sell."

"It could be mighty expensive to keep. The tax people are reassessing the whole county this year."

"You're a cheerful soul. . . ."

"And since the plywood plant is cutting their payroll, there'll be trouble anteing up those taxes. Most of the town eats on that company."

Her eyes darkened with anger. "Who in the world said anything about the plant payroll being cut?"

He shifted uneasily. "You know how it goes. A bartender at the Inn hears lots of things. You can't blame folks for being interested."

"I'm not blaming anybody, but it isn't true about the plant being in jeopardy." She absently scuffed a ditch in the sand with the toe of her shoe. "At the moment, the company is holding its own, mainly due to the increased Alaskan shipping."

"That's just a temporary shot in the arm."

"I know," she said patiently, "but at least it tides us over. Since I'm one of the major stockholders—thanks to my uncle—believe me, I'm interested too."

"Then why is Bart Winthrop coming to town?"

She smiled and shook her head. "Who knows? I just received his letter this morning . . . your grapevine has the C.I.A. beat all hollow."

"You'd be surprised the things I could tell you about this place."

"Well, spare me. But to set the story straight, Mr. Winthrop is probably coming because he's executor for my uncle's estate and has some papers for me to sign."

"And he hasn't said anything to you about closing down the plant?"

She put up her right hand in mock salute. "Scout's honor—not a word." Her tone softened. "Mr. Winthrop has even had some takeover offers for the company shares, so things can't be all bad." She gave him a level look. "It would help if you'd tell the men to stop worrying. We don't want labor troubles because of unfounded rumors."

"Okay." He scrubbed out his cigarette and watched her follow suit before burying both ends under a mound of sand. "I'll spread the word. Seems to me you have your hands full with that estate of your uncle's—what with Mr. Calhoun and his development company after you for the property and Mr. Winthrop bossing the plywood plant."

"I'll admit things were more peaceful when I worked in New Orleans." She smiled ruefully. "But my uncle wanted his estate to stay in the family and I'm the last of the line."

"Then you'd better find yourself a husband and start a new line. It won't be any trouble—not with your looks."

Her smile widened. "Those are the nicest words I've heard today. I promise you, Ernie—when I do, you'll be the first to know."

"That's the ticket. Dump all your problems on some poor guy. Then you can stay home and look beautiful."

"It's easy to see that you haven't heard of Women's Lib. . . ."

"Oh, I've heard of it," he said casually as he stooped to retrieve his chain saw, "but we haven't exactly endorsed their ideas in our tribal meetings."

"And somehow I don't think you will." She walked beside him to the driftwood log he was reducing to chunks. "You might fill up my woodshed one of these days when Mr. Calhoun leaves town again."

"Okay. It'll probably be the first of the week." He looked down the beach. "You'll have to step lively if you're going to get much of a walk—the tide's turned."

"I know. I'll be careful." She pulled a scarf from her jacket pocket and tied it over her hair. "See you later, Ernie."

"Right. Hey—in case anybody asks—what kind of odds should I give on Mr. Calhoun?"

"Better ask him. You wouldn't like the ones I'd

14

give you." She waved casually and set off down the beach.

The penetrating noise of Ernie's chain saw faded as her determined strides took her due north on the desolate expanse of sand that was Sea Bend's pride and joy. Massive piles of driftwood tangled in a natural bulkhead at the high tide mark by the foot of the steep cliffs to her right. Luxurious ocean-front homes were hidden in the heavy vegetation at the top of the cliffs leaving a deserted natural look on the beach itself. Her own home was located at the top of the highest rise, but all that was visible was the broad brick chimney and the reflection of light from the wide living room windows. The rest of the house with its weathered brown siding and silvery cedar shake roof camouflaged easily among the tall pines and verdant undergrowth.

As she walked on, the hill dipped sharply to reveal the outermost corner of her framed glass patio wall, which connected to the main body of the house on the ocean side. Smoke still eddied in gentle wisps from the barbecue fireplace, which doubled as an outdoor heater in the colder months. With the high glass patio wall to stop the prevailing Chinook wind and a brisk fire to provide a token warmth, it was possible for Jean to enjoy outdoor living during the early spring days when other Sea Bend residents still hovered inside over their furnace ducts.

She stopped for a minute to tighten the knot of her scarf and look over her shoulder at the threatening clouds to the south. The weather stations had primed coastal residents for a gusty downpour, and it looked as if they were right.

Their forecast made her hesitate before striding on toward the rocky outcropping ahead of her. If she had an iota of sense, she'd be hurrying to get back home before the rains came, but the prospect of another long evening in an empty living room made her keep doggedly on. After all, she reasoned, she wouldn't dissolve if she did get wet and she still had time for a quick look at the agate beds on the far side of Wailing Rock.

She glanced at her watch before clambering up the rock shelf with the rugged monolith at the end of it. Even if the tide was well-turned, she should have about fifteen minutes to make it back between the rocks. Any later and she'd face a steep winding hike around the hills behind her, since the only track was the one Rick rode down each day to deliver a paper to the new resident on the beach.

Not that she'd be welcome there. Residents of secluded beach cottages usually took their isolation seriously and were best left strictly alone. She could only hope that Toby had told his tenant the agate beds in front of the property were public domain.

Carefully she moved around the barnacle-covered tidal pools on the slippery rocks determined not to be distracted this time by the fascinating sea anemones in their depths. The rainbow-hued sea creatures held a lure for every beach lover, and residents, as well as visitors, were generally found crouched by the pools watching the graceful spines. In their retracted shapes, the anemones festooned the gray rocks like an abstract pattern on wallpaper—a marvelous slapdash design which testified to nature's genius.

One of Jean's shoes slipped on a loose rock and she sprawled forward onto her hands and knees. To her left, an incoming wave smashed on the side of the ledge and left her feeling as if she'd walked under the spray of a mammoth sprinkling bottle. As she stood up, her ankle twinged in protest.

"Damn! That's all I need right now," she said, leaning over to rub it. Standing erect again, she twisted her foot gingerly and found it didn't hurt if she treated it carefully.

She moved on . . . this time to the point of the promontory. Taking a deep breath, she squeezed through the aperture made by the cliff and the outthrust that was Wailing Rock itself. For a moment she remained spread-eagled, embracing the rock's clammy

16

sides with her arms wide and her nose pressed against the surface.

She edged through precariously. Only the rhythmic scrape of a breaker nibbling at the rocky ledge below disturbed the solitude. Just another foot or so now, she decided, retaining a handhold on the rock and backing carefully. Once her foot found the familiar crevice on the ledge, all she had to do was wait for the moment between waves and make a dash for the gravel beach.

Her questing toe suddenly found new territory.

"Hey—watch it!" said a deep surprised voice behind her.

Startled, she relaxed her grip and plummeted down the ledge onto the beach below. It was only a five-foot drop, but she landed hard on the ankle she had been favoring.

"Ouch!" she protested painfully.

"Look out!" The warning was sharp and the arms that reached down to gather her up were strong, but the incoming wave paid no attention to either and before she could gather her wits, Jean found herself spluttering in eight inches of surging salt water.

"Oh lord—what a mess!" She rolled onto her knees and started to get up.

"Take it easy. Hang onto me."

"You don't have to threaten me," she managed, clinging to the proffered arm and pulling herself up.

"I wasn't sure. Anybody who can't come off a rock without putting a foot in a man's face . . ."

She pulled to a limping stop halfway up the beach and stared at the tall figure by her side. For the first time she noted his level gray-eyed gaze, the straight, crisp dark hair topping a lean attractive profile, and the width of powerful shoulders accentuated by a wet flannel shirt.

"Did I do that? Oh heavens, I'm sorry." She moved forward again in response to an impatient tug. "I didn't expect to find anybody crouched at the bottom of Wailing Rock. What in the world were you hiding from?"

17

"I was *not* hiding." His deep voice had impatient undertones. "I was reaching down to pick up a dandy agate when you decided to drop in . . . literally." He stared disapprovingly down at her limping form. "It's no wonder you've hurt your foot—charging off a rock face like that."

She pulled up again, disregarding a new wave which was swirling coldly around her soggy shoes. "I was *not* charging! You startled me and when I slid down I landed on the ankle I'd twisted a few minutes ago." She watched his changing expression and took fresh umbrage. "And I was being careful then, too. It's just that those rocks are darned slippery."

"Well, I'm glad you've found it out. Teen-agers these days . . ."

"Teen-agers! Good heavens . . . I'm twenty-three, Mr. . . . er . . ."

"Stevenson." There was outright amusement in his look now. "Grant Stevenson." His gray eyes fixed on her more intently, taking in the pleasing figure revealed by the clinging white sweater. "I'm sorry. I didn't mean to insult you, Miss . . ." The glance switched abruptly to her left hand. "Miss? . . ."

"Cameron. Jean Cameron." She became conscious of her hair hanging in limp strands as it dripped salt water. "Rick told me about you," she added absently.

"Rick? Oh, you mean my paperboy?"

She nodded. "He mentioned an artist was living in Toby's cottage. I was hoping he'd told you that everyone looks for agates in these beds."

"That's fine with me. Look . . ." his grip on her elbow tightened, "maybe at twenty-three you're young enough to ignore this wind, but I'm thirty-four and it feels damn cold. Let's get up to the cabin."

Her head swiveled toward the big A-frame shelter near the shore as if she had just become aware of its existence. Standing in neat isolation among the tall spruce trees, the silvery shake roof of the structure took on the patina of old sterling in the gathering dusk.

"It isn't necessary," she said nervously. "If you'll

18

just give me a boost back through the rock, I can get back to my house. . . ."

"How? On your hands and knees?" The words were scathing. "I've heard about that mountain aerie of yours and I've noticed the path up to it. You'd never make it."

She took a step forward and felt a twinge of pain shoot up her instep. Unconsciously she grabbed for the support of his arm. "You win. I suppose I can call someone to come and get me."

There was a brief hesitation before he said, "I suppose so."

"Well, in that case," she managed a thin smile which twisted as she sneezed sharply, "you have an unexpected gift from the sea."

"Someone said to 'enjoy the gifts that fortune sends.' " He watched her search her jacket pockets and then pulled a clean but damp handkerchief from his hip pocket. "Here—be my guest. You'll have to wring it out first."

She took it and blew her nose thankfully.

"Ready?" He seemed oblivious to anything unusual in the situation.

"I guess so." That assured manner of his was beginning to have a disastrous effect on her heartbeat. "If I can borrow your arm until we get to the cabin . . ."

He ignored her words and, reaching over, swung her effortlessly in his arms and started up the beach.

"But you don't have to . . ." her protest trailed off as she realized he wasn't paying any attention to her. Finally she managed to say primly, "I hope you don't get the wrong idea of Sea Bend from all this."

"My God, you sound like the set of rules put out by Toby's corporation. Even the fishing laws are framed and mounted in my utility room." He grinned down at her. "You don't have to worry—I know all the restrictions on taking anything from the sea. No license needed but make sure you throw the under-sized ones back in."

"What does that have to do with me?"

"I thought you were concerned." His tone was judi-

19

cious. "After all, at twenty-three, you're a strictly legal catch and I wouldn't have to give you up." He grinned again. "Fortunately for you, Miss Cameron, I've never cared much for fishing."

Chapter *TWO*

———◆————◆————◆———

Toby's development corporation hadn't stinted in furnishing Grant's A-frame retreat. This was evident from Jean's first glimpse of the interior. A natural linen drapery in gold, black, and brown was hanging at the long windows and a comfortable L-shaped davenport fronted the raised circular fireplace at one end of the spacious living area.

She protested as Grant pushed open the sliding window at the front of the cabin. "Don't take me through the living room—I'll drip all over your carpet."

"Don't be silly." He edged through the opening into the comforting warmth of the house. "Toby assured me it's the indoor-outdoor variety and practically indestructible."

Jean looked dubiously down at the dark brown pile beneath his feet. "Well, I'd still feel better dripping on a kitchen floor."

"We'd better make that a bathroom floor. The kitchen is pretty much out in the open here." He put her down and led the way toward the rear of the cottage. "The only room with four honest-to-God walls is the bathroom. Even the most modern architects haven't taken any liberties with it." He opened the door with a flourish. "It's all yours."

"And very nice too. Some hot water will feel good." She admired the room's hickory paneling above beige fixtures. Deep orange towels and curtains provided a cheerful accent color.

"It's going to take more than hot water," Grant said carelessly. "Peel down and I'll find you something dry to wear." He closed the door and left her staring in consternation at his green silk robe hanging from a hook on the back of it.

A wave of color spread over her cheeks as she took in its implications. Evidently Grant Stevenson was accustomed to moving swiftly where his female visitors were concerned, although he hadn't seemed the type. Despite that frivolous comment about the spoils of the sea, she hadn't felt alarmed at being alone with him until now.

She fingered the robe nervously. What a pity it wasn't wool, so she could put it on over her damp blouse for extra warmth. Slowly she unzipped her windbreaker and laid it on a hamper by the window. If she could get rid of her chill with hot water and a good rubdown—her clothes could dry on her. Grant would find that she didn't need his robe at all.

"Hey—it's mighty quiet in there." His voice from the other side of the door jerked her to attention. "Get in that hot shower or you'll have pneumonia."

"That won't be necessary. . . ."

"Stick an arm out . . ." he went on, obviously not hearing her murmured response, "and you can try these clothes on for size. I'm sorry I don't have anything better."

Jean stared at her reflection in the mirror of the medicine cabinet. Then abruptly she went over to the door and opened it—just far enough to accept the bundle of clothing he thrust at her. "Thank you," she said in a subdued voice.

"No trouble," he replied casually.

"You must be wanting to change too."

"I was on my way upstairs."

She became aware of his annoyed glance. "Is something wrong?"

"Not really. I just can't understand why you're still hanging around in those wet clothes."

She backed hurriedly. "Sorry." There was no point in explaining why it had taken her so long to reach her present state of undress. "I won't be long now."

He paused in the act of closing the door. "There's no hurry once you get dry again. I put the kettle on to boil so if you beat me, you can pour the water through the filter in the coffeepot. You'll find everything on the stove."

"All right . . . thanks."

This time his definite closing of the door punctuated her words and she turned happily back to see what she was clutching in the way of a wardrobe change. Grant had unearthed a pair of well-worn beige corduroy pants and threaded a length of quarter-inch nylon rope through the belt tabs to help her keep them up. There were two thick wool hunting socks which would have to serve as slippers as well. The beige-and-rust-colored wool shirt looked both comfortable and expensive. All in all, she decided, a very satisfactory outfit.

Putting her loot carefully on a bath stool in the corner of the room, she started peeling off her wet things noting that her nylon underwear was already half dry.

While she was waiting to get the proper warm water mixture in the shower, she caught a brief glimpse of herself in the mirror. Not too bad, she thought judiciously. That is, if anyone preferred a shapely woman slightly on the blue side.

The shower felt just as good as she had imagined. She luxuriated in the hot needle-spray until she felt the blood coursing through her body and then gradually finished by letting tepid water slide over her. It took all her willpower to finally turn off the taps and start toweling herself dry. Then she hurriedly donned her borrowed clothing and found a small towel to wipe the steam off the mirror so she could survey her appearance.

She smiled as she noted the turned-up shirt sleeves and pleated trouser waistband. To think she had worried about Grant making a pass at her! That idea couldn't have entered his mind when he had selected those clothes.

She raked her fingers through her newly shampooed hair, uttering a silent word of thanks that there was enough natural wave in it to withstand a ducking and still emerge fairly presentable. She peered earnestly in the mirror again. Since lipstick wasn't available, she'd just have to present a shiny, well-scrubbed appearance and hope that it would pass.

Gathering up her soggy clothes, she opened the bathroom door and peered around the edge of it. She could hear the kettle singing on the stove, so Grant must still be changing.

"Hi! Did you finally get warm?" He came into the short hall behind her.

"Oh . . ." Startled, she spun to face him. "Yes, thanks."

"Let me take those wet things."

She relinquished the damp bundle gladly. "I was wondering what to do with them."

"I'll hang them in the utility room, but it may take a while. . . ."

"Don't worry," she told him reassuringly. "If I don't present too horrible a spectacle in these trousers of yours, I'm happy to be warm and dry."

"On the contrary, I didn't know those cords had such possibilities." His eyebrows rose in amusement. "You definitely add something to the landscape."

She kept a solemn expression as she surveyed her ankles. "I thought the footwear was especially fetching."

They both stared at the drooping wool socks.

Grant said, "If Yves St. Laurent could see you, he'd start a new trend."

"Yves St. Laurent would run screaming from the room."

"Forget it. I only let the French influence me on vintage wines and sauce Béarnaise. Speaking of food . . ."

24

"I'm on my way to make the coffee now," she said taking the hint.

"Good. Look through the refrigerator while I'm hanging out the wash. My stomach says it's dinnertime."

When he came back, he found her hanging over the stove sniffing beatifically at the aroma of freshly brewed coffee. "What's the menu?" he asked.

"Unless you want to wait for things to thaw . . . waffles and bacon are the best bet."

"Waffles and bacon will be fine." He gave her a quizzical look. "Is it any use hoping that you're a *cordon bleu* chef as well as a leader of French fashion?"

"I can keep us from starving to death," she said dryly. Moving toward the refrigerator, she added, "From the look of your larder, you don't often eat at home."

"Not any more than I have to," he admitted cheerfully, taking a pound of bacon and a carton of eggs from her and putting them on the copper-tiled counter.

"Yet you have a kitchen that looks like a magazine illustration." She gestured toward the matching copper-colored appliances which blended pleasantly with the light wood cabinets above them.

"Evidently Toby hired a good decorator. I just happened onto a great vacation spot."

She added a container of milk to the provisions on the counter and reached into a cupboard for a mixing bowl. "This is the first time Toby has ever rented the cottage. Generally, it's kept for V.I.P. friends of his. . . ." She broke off, flushing. "I'm sorry, that was tactless of me. Are you. . . ?"

He shook his head. "Definitely not. Toby and I are strictly chance acquaintances. We have a mutual friend who suggested I get in touch with him."

Jean stared at him momentarily and then dropped her gaze back to the mixing bowl. From his expression, it was evident that the "mutual friend" was female and a close acquaintance rather than a chance one. If the "friend" was known to Toby, she probably had an impressive bank balance as well. Just the

25

kind of patron that an artist needed. She stared unseeingly at the eggbeater on the counter top and uttered a soft sigh.

Grant snapped his fingers. "Have you gone into a brown study?"

"Certainly not," she said crossly. "Make yourself useful and fry the bacon."

His black eyebrows climbed slightly at her tone, but he only frowned briefly at the top of her bent head and said, "Right. I'll take care of it."

There was no further conversation until Jean had prepared the waffle batter and set two places at the small formica table near the stove.

"I think that's everything," she said finally. "Sit down and start on your grapefruit while I put the batter in for your waffle." She watched him pull back a chair and then asked, "Am I interfering with any plans you had for the evening?"

"No, you aren't changing a thing." He picked up his grapefruit spoon. "I was already committed to an evening at home before you dropped in."

"That's one way of describing my arrival. Did you have any company coming?"

He shook his head. "No company—either coming or going. What I meant was that my car is sitting out in the carport with an empty gas tank." He concentrated on the fruit in front of him and avoided her gaze. "They forgot to fill it up when it was in for servicing this morning. When the fellow dropped it off this afternoon, he had to coast the last fifty feet. Fortunately, he had a service station pickup to get him back. Since I didn't have any plans for the evening, I told them not to make a special trip with the gas—just have somebody drop it off when they were going by."

"But good heavens . . . on this road . . . that could be days."

"It's not as isolated as that. Rick comes every afternoon with the paper and there are a couple of cars a day heading for the agate beaches north of here."

She chewed on her lower lip. "It's too late now to get back around the Rock. . . ."

"And you're not in any condition to hike up the beach even if you could get around it," he said definitely. "Besides, the fellow from the gas station knows I have an appointment in town tomorrow morning, so he's bound to drop off some gas before then." He finished the grapefruit and carried his plate over to the counter. "Aren't you going to eat?"

"In a minute," she said absently. "You'd better start on your waffle." She extracted it deftly and put it on a warmed plate. "I'll pour your coffee."

"Okay . . . but by rights I should be waiting on you."

"Don't be silly. This is the least I can do." She watched him settle in his place before saying doubtfully, "Well, I suppose there should be some transportation by morning although . . ." She looked up in relief. "For heaven's sake, there's no need to bother you. I can phone for a cab. . . ." Her words trailed off as he shook his head. "No cab?" she asked finally.

"No telephone. One of the charms of the cottage. That's a direct quote from your friend Toby." He took a bite of waffle. "I don't mean to sound ungallant but it's two and a half miles to the main road."

"In the dark and"—she cocked her head to listen —"in the rain."

"Exactly. Unless you need urgent medical attention for your ankle, it would be a hell of a lot more convenient if you'd consider yourself a guest until they drop off the gasoline." He held up a hand as she started to interrupt. "I know we weren't properly introduced, but I can assure you that waffles don't inspire me to anything more strenuous than a game of cribbage in front of the fireplace." He grinned slightly. "Despite that glamorous costume of yours."

She strove for a casual tone. "Unfortunately I don't play cribbage."

"Chess then?"

"Would you settle for gin rummy?"

"Gin rummy it is. Even Amy Vanderbilt couldn't

27

object to that. I'll take over the cooking now." He rinsed his empty plate in the sink. "Go ahead and eat your grapefruit."

It wasn't until later and Jean was pouring syrup on her waffle that he spoke again.

"Miss Cameron . . . "

"Jean, please," she corrected automatically.

"Jean . . . there is one thing I'd like to ask you."

The hesitancy in his tone made her look up quickly. All of her suspicions came surging to the fore again as she stared at his tall figure leaning against the counter. Even wearing another well-worn flannel shirt and a pair of suntans, there was an assurance about him. With that dark brown—almost black—hair slicked crisply back and tanned skin stretched tightly over high cheekbones and aquiline nose, he looked like the profile on an ancient Roman coin. And at the moment, he was surveying her with the same intent look those emperors had cast over their captive females.

She put the syrup pitcher down carefully in the exact center of its saucer. Grant Stevenson could entertain any ideas of grandeur that he chose, but he'd better learn she wasn't part of the loot to be divided.

"I doubt if I can be of any help," she said with icicles dripping. "Exactly what did you have in mind?"

One of those thick eyebrows went up again. "To be specific," he replied just as testily, "the garbage collection at Sea Bend."

"Garbage collection. . . ?" she whispered inanely.

"Precisely." His sharp glance cut her down to size. "I wanted to know the schedule, but I'll call Toby tomorrow when I'm in town."

"No! I know all . . . " She found herself pouring a second layer of syrup on an already inundated waffle and dropped the pitcher noisily down again. "The collecting is done Monday morning in this part of town," she said, trying to pull her thoughts back to normal and feeling all kinds of a fool. "Could I help? I mean . . ."

"I don't expect you to lend a hand." He was obviously trying to fathom the reason for her incoherence. "It was just that nobody had shown up and I wondered if you had to be a special friend of the mayor." He waved a casual hand toward the sink. "Most of the stuff goes down the disposal or in the fireplace, but the tin cans are a problem."

"How have you managed them so far?"

"By digging up half the hillside and burying them. . . ." He broke off as he saw her lean on the table, convulsed with laughter. "I know it sounds silly. Maybe I should rent a goat."

"No . . . not that." She barely managed to get the words out through the paroxysms of merriment. "I'm sorry . . . but I can just see you stealing out in the middle of the night distributing empty soup cans at trash barrels all along the Oregon coast."

"I told you I was desperate. It almost seemed easier to find another place to live."

"That's cheating. Like buying a new stove rather than cleaning the oven of your old one." She mopped her eyes with the back of her hand. "If you'll get in touch with Toby's secretary, she'll make proper arrangements right away. In the meantime, feel free to use my garbage cans."

"Thanks—that's the best offer I've had today. I'll hold you to it." He glanced down at her plate. "If you've had enough of that waffle, let's take our coffee in by the fireplace."

She nodded. "I think I will give up. There's so much syrup on it that it's like being treated for shock. What about the dishes?"

"Forget about them. I may not be much on solving garbage problems, but I'm a topnotch dishwasher and I only work in the forenoon."

"In that case," she told him moving toward the living room, "you can invite me to dinner anytime."

He switched out the kitchen light. "Women! Whoever called them the weaker sex?"

"An unmarried man, I imagine." She sat down on the davenport and put her coffee mug on a convenient end table. Absently she watched him gather paper and kindling to start a fire in the raised fireplace nearby. "I was hoping you'd think of that," she confessed as he struck a match and fed the flames carefully. "That's all this room needs to make it perfect."

She let her gaze wander over the high-ceilinged room with its easy chairs and low, well-filled bookcases near the long windows. At the far side, a spiral stair led to the balcony above where the bedroom evidently was located.

Grant moved over to pull the linen draperies, shutting out the turbulence of the rainy night and isolating the cottage into a cocoon of warmth and comfort. "If you look again, you'll find the lived-in look," he invited, gesturing toward an unadorned glass gallon jar full of water on a fruitwood end table. Inside, a bedraggled goldfish was swimming listlessly round the container's curved sides. "Homer," Grant said laconically.

Jean moved over to take a closer look.

As a denizen of the deep, Homer appeared an apathetic afterthought. His fins were ragged and his scales could have used a new paint job.

"Where did you get him . . . a month-end sale?" she asked.

"Hardly. He was a housewarming present."

"Of course! Rick!"

"Right the first time. He thought I needed company. I had my choice of Homer or Max."

"His four-foot iguana?"

He nodded grimly. "Homer was definitely the better bargain."

"Rick is having a little trouble placing Max," she said carefully.

"Umm." The monosyllable spoke volumes. "I thought he might."

Jean glanced again at the feebly swimming Homer. "Maybe he's lonesome. Have you thought of supplying a friend for him?"

"No—but it has crossed my mind to dispose of Homer. Unfortunately Rick checks on his progress every day."

30

"When faced with the inevitable . . ."

"Relax and enjoy it. I know. And knowing Rick— I'll probably end up taking Homer back to Los Angeles in a fancy twelve-gallon tank."

She smiled. "You'll come to love him like a brother."

"That'll be the day." He finished piling wood on the fire and dusted his hands on his trouser legs. "Want some more coffee?"

"No thanks. This is a delightful place. How would you like to swap houses sight unseen?"

Grant pulled up an easy chair and sat down. "From what I hear, I'd be getting the better deal."

"For a new resident, you're remarkably well informed."

"Two unimpeachable reference sources," he confirmed. "Rick is a bottomless well of information and Ernie, the bartender at the Inn. . . ."

"Say no more."

"You don't have to worry. They're both admirers of yours."

She grinned wryly. "I won't believe everything I hear about you if you promise not to believe everything you hear about me."

"It's a deal . . . but I can't see why anyone would be interested in me."

"You underestimate Sea Bend." She held up her fingers and ticked them off. "First, you've arrived out-of-season; second, you're in Toby's special cottage; third, you're an artist, so maybe you're famous. . . ." She glanced around the walls. "Although there isn't any evidence of your work—not an easel in sight."

"How about the bucket of paint on the back porch?"

"Ummm. Secretive too." She settled on the davenport and pushed a cushion behind her. "Rick will have to probe further."

"You already know more than I do," Grant complained and ticked off his own list. "First, you live in a showplace on top of the hill that you inherited from your uncle. Second, you're unmarried, but Toby Calhoun has a corner on the market. . . ."

"You've been listening to Ernie."

31

"Third, as well as owning that sizable chunk of real estate, you're one of the main stockholders in the plywood plant at the edge of town."

"Another inheritance from my uncle."

"Don't interrupt. Fourth, although you're not a native, you've been a frequent visitor to Sea Bend and you gave up a public relations job in New Orleans to come back here. What's puzzling most of the population is whether you're going to stay around." He leaned back in his chair and grinned. "Are you?"

She raised her coffee mug in mock salute to the bald query. "Maybe, maybe not."

"Don't be polite. Tell me to mind my own business."

"I promise to let you and Ernie know when I decide." Her joking tone sobered. "What you don't know is that I have to stay here two more months to inherit under the terms of my uncle's will. Either that —or get married"—she flicked him a quick glance— "to a solvent, employed male who meets with the executor's approval."

He whistled softly. "What happens then?"

"Then . . . presumably my poor husband would take over. My uncle was a great believer in masculine superiority."

He felt in his shirt pocket for a package of cigarettes and leaned forward to offer her one. "Well, nobody's twisting your arm to get married," he said calmly. "You can sit by yourself on the top of the hill and cock a snook at the whole bunch." He watched her move restlessly and narrowed his eyes. "Or can't you?"

"You are the most curious man. . . ." she burst out.

"Sorry. I didn't mean to . . ."

"No, *I'm* sorry. Actually, you managed to hit a sensitive spot." The words came out slowly. "I've been wondering all afternoon how to get out of a difficult situation. A . . . friend of mine . . . is getting too serious. I don't want to hurt his feelings, but I'd like to make things clear. Normally, I'd go away for a while, but under the terms of my uncle's will, I have to stay at Sea Bend and this . . . friend . . . can be very persuasive." She looked up and met his eyes. "Frankly, it's a mess."

He nodded understandingly. "Toby can't take 'no' for an answer, I gather."

Her cheeks flamed. "Was I so obvious? Sorry—I shouldn't have been spouting off. It's just that I don't have anyone to talk to and since you're a stranger . . ."

"And not involved—you could tell me. I understand. Stop writhing." He frowned suddenly. "Maybe I can even help."

She looked up. "How?"

He leaned forward to put his lighter to the tip of her cigarette and lit his own before answering. "I plan to be at Sea Bend for about three weeks. You and I could discover that we're old acquaintances and I could take you around occasionally." He gave her a quizzical look to see what effect his words were having. "That's if you care for the idea. As far as Toby Calhoun goes—you can make whatever explanation you like. Either put him off gently or firmly . . . that's up to you. As far as your executor is concerned, he has no reason to be critical of your acquaintances until you plan to marry one." A grin slashed across his tanned face. "It's a good thing we're not serious. I can see you explaining an . . . artist . . . as a solvent, wage-earning husband."

"Bart would certainly dig in his toes on that," she admitted, considering his offer. "If you're serious, we could try it for a week or so. It might be a terrific help. Are you sure that it wouldn't inconvenience you?"

"It wouldn't. As a matter of fact, you'd be doing me a favor too."

"Oh? How could that be?"

"Well . . ." he drawled the word out to two syllables, "to make a long story very short—I'd like to discourage a young lady."

Her eyes widened. "I see."

"I'm not sure that you do." He was evidently determined to be fair about things. "She's serious—I'm not. It's embarrassing because she's the friend who recommended Sea Bend for my vacation. I received

33

a letter today saying that she's planning a holiday here herself—she's accompanying her guardian or something like that." He reached over and ground out his cigarette with a decisive gesture. "I'm in the same fix you're in with Toby Calhoun. I don't want to hurt her feelings, so . . ."

"If I could hang around the fringes, she might understand that you aren't ready to settle down."

"Exactly."

"That shouldn't be hard. Shall we form a mutual benefit society?"

"You make it sound like the Worshipful Society of Vintners," he complained, "but that's the general idea." He reached over to pull a small table between them and extracted a deck of cards from the drawer of it. "Let's play gin rummy or you'll be falling asleep before I can make you pay for your supper."

"You're right. It's the combination of the fireplace fire and the fresh air." She pushed back a strand of hair from her forehead. "How expensive are your waffle dinners?"

"It depends," he said, shuffling the deck. "In this case, the loser can buy a drink tomorrow night—provided you let me take you out to dinner afterwards."

"Sold!" She studied his face while he was intent upon dealing. The assurance was back in his manner, she decided. Not that he had been without it for long. That strong jaw line and determined chin didn't fit with any of her preconceived ideas about creative artists. His hands looked more suited to grasping a tennis racket than a palette and the strong shoulders could have belonged to a longshoreman. But his quiet sense of humor and steady glance had revealed more of his personality than any outward physical characteristics. For a moment she felt only sympathy for that woman he wanted to discourage . . . and it was obvious from Grant's manner that she wasn't the first who had received the offhand treatment.

She watched him turn and put a log on the fire after he finished dealing the cards. It would be interesting, she decided, to know more about him.

34

"At this rate, you'll never win that drink." His voice prodded her gently.

She came quickly back to earth and picked up her hand. "The dickens I won't. What are the house rules? Deuces wild and triple score for one-eyed jacks?"

"Play cards, madame. You can play spit-in-the-ocean another day."

She shook her head sadly. "No sense of humor. I can see I'll have to cheat very carefully."

Three games later found Grant ahead by 150 points and Jean half-asleep on the couch.

"That's enough for tonight," he told her as he tallied the score. "You can settle your debts tomorrow. Being a man of honor, I won't insist on an I.O.U." He looked at his watch. "Evidently the gas will be delivered on the swing shift. You'd better rest while we're waiting. I'll get a blanket and you can stay there on the davenport if you like."

"But what about you?"

"My bedroom's on the balcony." He was amused at her suddenly wary expression. "If it makes you feel easier, I only plan to lie on top of the bed and read for a while. That way, I'll be awake when they deliver the gas and I can get you home before dawn." He was pulling an extra pillow and blanket out of the hall linen closet as he spoke. "There's a new toothbrush in the bathroom if you want to borrow it. You can have first turn in there while I'm fixing the couch." He frowned as she moved to pass him. "That outfit of yours doesn't look very comfortable to rest in. If you like, you can borrow that robe of mine that's hanging on the door." He turned dismissingly and tossed the pillow casually toward the far end of the davenport. "I'll wake you when the car's ready."

She hovered in the hall. "If you're sure . . ."

"It's strictly up to you. Turn off the hall light if you don't want it shining in your eyes."

If he had been less determined or evinced the slightest interest in her activities, Jean would never have shed the wool shirt and bulky corduroys to slip into his dressing gown. She hesitated even as she

35

reached for it on the hook. Then overhead she heard the slight creak of springs as Grant settled on his bed. Obviously he was a man of his word. Not only that but he was busily extricating himself from any matrimonial hopes his "friend" might have, so he was hardly in the position to be looking for another entanglement. She reached for the robe and slipped it on without another qualm.

When she got back to the living room, the only real light was the flickering of the fire. A soft glow on the cathedral ceiling indicated that Grant was reading as he had planned.

Jean slid gratefully under the blanket on the wide couch and let her body relax on the cushions. Even the pillow was just right; not the kind that fought back nor collapsed like a leaky balloon. Her eyelids flickered once . . . twice . . . and then forgot to flicker again.

When the noise came later, Jean struggled up on an elbow. Then, still half asleep, she stumbled to her feet wondering what had wakened her. Finally it came again—a soft knock penetrating just enough to rouse her. By that time she was aware that it came from the back door.

As groggy as a prizefighter on the final count, she headed for the hallway, pulling the dressing gown tightly round her to keep from tripping on its length.

There was no thought to her action as she turned the doorknob. Someone knocked—she was answering. It was merely a conditioned reflex and nothing more.

It wasn't until the cold outside air hit her face when she pulled open the door that her mind really started to function. By the time she recognized an astounded Ernie Ravenwing standing there with an emergency gas can in his hand, she became horrifyingly aware of the picture she presented.

In case she was in any doubt, each of the expressions that went over Ernie's face as he noted her tousled hair and the masculine robe clutched so tightly around her body would have convinced her.

It seemed an age before he shoved the gas can toward her like an unwanted child. "I guess you were expecting this," he mumbled uneasily, "or Mr. Stevenson was." He stepped backward. "I won't hang around to give it to him. See ya around, Jean." He managed to get back into his dune buggy and drive off without looking her way again.

Jean stood transfixed in the doorway. She was still there when Grant came up behind her saying, "Who the hell was that?"

She let her hand slip nervelessly from the doorknob and turned to present him with the gas can. "A Mr. Ravenwing—bearing gifts. He came to call on you, but he left convinced that he'd interrupted Sea Bend's newest and finest orgy." She shook her head wearily. "By the time Ernie gets through spreading the story I suspect we'll get more coverage than the dead whale that washed ashore last month."

Chapter *THREE*

———◆◆◆——

The memory of Ernie's unexpected call might not have been so bad, Jean decided, if Grant had only taken it more seriously. For a man whose reputation had just been blasted, he was patently unconcerned.

He had merely plucked the gas can from her hand, told her to get dressed, and twenty minutes later had dropped her at her front porch with the reminder that he would pick her up at six that night.

In the pale morning light, she watched his car disappear down her steep drive. The red taillight flickered once when he applied his brakes at the main road and then flashed in a right-turn signal which meant that Mr. Stevenson was heading for town rather than back to his cabin retreat.

"Probably on his way to breakfast," Jean said to herself as she fumbled for her key and pushed open the heavy front door. The thought of food made her pause momentarily by the kitchen before she surrendered to weariness and proceeded down the long hall to her bedroom.

Its yellow and white freshness seemed more welcoming than ever after her disturbed night and she detoured just far enough to wash her face in the adjoining bath before undressing and staggering toward the king-sized bed. As she left her still-damp and wrinkled clothes on the bathroom hamper, she thought it was a pity she couldn't abandon all memories of the previous night in the same way.

Those vivid memories were still rankling when she finally awoke at noon. It took a minute to realize that it wasn't her guilty conscience bothering her, but the sound of a vacuum cleaner being pushed noisily down the hall outside her door.

Her forehead cleared as she remembered that her cleaning woman had planned to put in some extra hours during the week.

"The house needs a real good rubbin' up," the older woman had said. "When Mr. Winthrop comes to town you'll be doin' some entertaining and we'd better be ready."

Jean decided she was scarcely doing her part by lying in bed until noon and swung her feet to the floor. She walked over to the wide window which looked out on the ocean view.

Last night's storm had evidently moved up the coast. Down below the tide was on its way out and the beach stretched wide and inviting in the clear spring sunshine.

She pulled back a sheer ruffled curtain and glanced down where Wailing Rock stood in solitary grandeur. There wasn't a flicker of movement on the sand around it. Not that she had really expected anything else. Evidently Grant didn't bother to stir from his own stretch of beach on the other side.

Outside her room, the vacuum was switched off and a peremptory knock came on the door.

"Miss Jean—you up yet?" Mrs. Lloyd's flat twang still bore semblances of a New England upbringing. "I want to vacuum the bedrooms."

"I'm just on my way to the shower," Jean called to assure her.

"That's good." There was an audible sniff. Cleanliness and early rising were linked to Godliness in Mrs. Lloyd's sphere. "Mr. Calhoun called to say he'd be round in about fifteen minutes. I'll make the coffee now. Sure hate to have him think we're just stirring." Her words faded as she started down the hall.

"Thank you, Mrs. Lloyd." The expression on Jean's face belied her polite response and she turned decisively toward the bathroom. A before-breakfast interview with Toby was unthinkable—she needed all her faculties when she talked to him. If he had caught wind of Ernie's visit, it would be doubly bad. By hurrying, she could manage one fortifying cup of coffee before he appeared.

Her timing was remarkably good. Toby's bright red MG came into view under her kitchen window just as she was finishing it.

The doorbell chimes cut into Mrs. Lloyd's tuneless humming as she dusted in the living room.

Jean saw her straighten and said hastily, "Never mind, Mrs. Lloyd. I'll get it." She hurried to the front door before Toby could ring again.

"Good morning . . . good morning," he caroled cheerfully as she pulled it open. "Lovely morning or . . ." he hesitated and glanced at his watch, "is it afternoon?"

"If it isn't—it soon will be," she admitted. "Come in, Toby, and share some coffee."

"The very reason I came." He was immaculate, as usual, in white golf slacks and a pale yellow sweater shirt. "Good morning, Mrs. Lloyd." He beamed on the gray-haired woman, who stopped dusting to nod as he went by.

"Morning, Mr. Calhoun. Hope you enjoy the coffee. I made it special—just the way you like."

"Good! You make the best coffee in town," he assured her before following Jean into the kitchen.

"Let's take it outside," she said, stacking china and silver, "if it's warm enough."

"Plenty—behind those glass walls of yours." He lifted the tray of coffee things leaving a plate of sweet rolls for her to carry. "Can you manage the sliding door?"

She nodded, pulling back the glass door leading

directly from the sunny kitchen out onto the patio. "Put the tray on the round table and I'll pull up the chairs." She deposited the plate of pastries on the table and brought up two raffia captain's chairs while he was pouring the coffee.

"I think that's everything," she said, sitting down at his side. "No it isn't . . . I forgot the napkins."

"Skip them," he put out a hand as she half-rose to her feet. "You can always borrow my handkerchief. Your coffee will get cold."

"That wouldn't be catastrophic," she protested but settled obediently back down, "despite your malarkey about how good it is."

"Mrs. Lloyd's a good old soul and there's no harm in buttering her up a bit."

Jean leaned back in her chair and smiled impishly. "It isn't necessary. Most women take a look at you and then fall all over themselves."

"Present company excepted, I gather."

"Ummm, I refuse to comment on that." She gazed at him consideringly, noting the sun-bleached fair hair which contrasted so favorably with his tanned skin. "Maybe you're a throwback to some old Norse god."

"A splinter on the family tree? Better ask my mother," he replied, calmly reaching for another roll. "These are good. Want to play some golf with me?"

"Today?" Her eyebrows rose. "Why aren't you working?"

"I can't win with you. If I try to tend to business— you complain that I'm too stiff-necked," he gave her a whimsical sideways glance, "so I've decided to try new tactics."

"You're up to something, Toby. What is it this time?"

"Not real estate," he mumbled through a bite of roll, "er . . . not exactly."

"I thought so. . . ."

He shook his head vigorously and swallowed some coffee. "It's not what you mean, Jeanie. I'm trying to break some bad news gently. There was another fire in the plywood plant early this morning."

41

"Oh no!"

"It's all right—nothing serious." He waved a placating hand. "Foster was on the telephone to me. The early shift caught it while it was still smoldering."

"Where was it this time?"

"Next to the plugging machine. There was some waste in an overturned metal container that the operator says shouldn't have been there. Fortunately, whoever left it made a mistake on the flammability potential." He reached for the coffee pot and refilled their cups. "It didn't do anything other than smudge the walls and make an almighty smell."

She hunched forward over the table and thoughtfully rested her chin on her hand. "Last month that faulty thermostat on the drying ovens practically gave Fred Foster another heart attack."

Toby nodded. "At least he was there to spot the trouble. That's what plant superintendents get paid for."

"I suppose so, but with these continued nearmisses, I'm about to have a heart attack myself."

"Yeah . . . I know." He pulled a clean handkerchief from his pocket and rubbed off his fingers. "The communal napkin," he told her, leaving it by the tray. "Want a cigarette?"

"No, thanks."

He lit his and tossed the match into the brick barbecue fireplace before saying, "The worst part about these plant flare-ups is that they upset everybody. Foster has hired an extra man on security because the employees are beginning to think the place is jinxed. You know what that kind of thinking can do to production."

She nodded.

"As soon as you have internal problems in business," he went on, "it starts showing up on the balance sheets. You can bet that's why Bart Winthrop is hotfooting it up here to look after his interests."

"You're right." She chewed on her lower lip. "As major stockholders, we'll be given another lecture on why it's better to sell out our interests at this time."

Her chair scraped on the patio floor as she shoved it back and stood up. "My dear executor isn't subtle on that score."

"Bart Winthrop didn't amass his fortune by being subtle. He has more interests than a rabbit has relatives and you can't blame him for wanting to protect his bank balance. I'm not sure that he isn't right about the plant. Maybe we would do better to sell out to those Midwestern interests he's always talking about."

Jean shoved her hands deep in the pockets of her denim skirt. "I just can't, Toby," she told him finally. "My uncle started that mill; half the town of Sea Bend lives on it. Who knows what would happen to the local payroll if we sold out?" She scuffed the sole of her tennis shoe along the edge of a brick as she added, "But I know that I haven't any right to try and influence you."

"Sure you have, Jeanie, every right in the world." He tossed his cigarette into the fireplace and came over to put a comforting arm around her shoulders. "Just say the word and I'll sign over my shares in the plant as a wedding present to you. Then you can tell Bart to fly back south and tend to his other companies. How's that for a business proposition?"

"Much too generous," she said flippantly. "I couldn't take advantage of you so early in the day."

"I know what I'm offering. When I called to take you out to dinner last night, I had even planned to throw in the offer of a North Cape cruise for a honeymoon." He shot her a quick glance. "By the way, where did you get to? There still wasn't any answer when I called again at ten." He pulled his chair around and sat back down.

"Checking up on me?" She kept her amused tone with an effort. "We didn't have a date and Ernie told me you had gone up the coast."

"He told me that you'd gone for a walk on the beach."

She frowned as suspicion made a tight ball in her stomach. "When did you see Ernie?"

"Last night, of course. I stopped at the Inn for a

43

drink after dinner. My dialing finger was worn to a stub by then. Where were you?" he asked again.

Her shrug concealed her relief. "Having dinner with your tenant."

"My tenant? Do you mean Stevenson?" His eyes narrowed. "I didn't know you were acquainted."

"We met some time ago," she evaded. "I'm surprised you rented your favorite cottage to a virtual stranger."

"He came highly recommended. Besides, he seems decent enough."

"I didn't think you liked artistic types."

"What does that have to do with it? There are types . . . and types, I guess. How did we get on the subject of Stevenson anyhow? What happened to my proposal . . . *this* time?" he added with heavy sarcasm.

She shook her head slowly and then turned her back to stare out at the ocean. "Sorry, Toby. About all we have in common are some shares in a plywood mill and a fondness for ocean-front land." She heard a muttered protest but went on doggedly. "Once the honeymoon cruise was over, we'd wake up one morning deciding we'd run out of conversation. I'll even be honest and say that you'd get bored first." Her lips quirked gently. "A few months from now, you'll be thanking the fates for your lucky escape."

He gave her a brief, unyielding stare before pushing back his chair and saying, "I don't give up that easily, Jean. Let's drop it for now, though. Going golfing with me?"

"I'm sorry. This afternoon is my volunteer stint at the hospital."

"Are you still pushing that library cart around the halls?"

"I have to do something," she countered. "Since I inherited this," she made a jerky gesture toward the house, "I can scarcely go into the village and ask for a job. And since your darned development company wouldn't approve of my scrounging driftwood, I'm delighted to have a volunteer job at the hospital." She grimaced. "I can't even stay home and clean house. Mrs. Lloyd has done that for twenty years and she needs the job."

"You could always go down and file for unemployment."

"Thanks heaps."

"I can see you're all set to be difficult," he said in aggrieved masculine fashion, "so I'll find someone else to go around with me at the golf club. What time do you want to have dinner?"

Her hand flew up to her mouth. "Oh lord, did we have a date?"

"Not a formal one. Why? Can't you make that either?"

"I'm sorry, Toby. I've made other plans."

"Damn!" He paused in the middle of sliding back a section of glass windbreak that faced onto the drive. "Since when do we need to make appointments. I took it for granted . . ."

"That's where you made your mistake," she put in gently. "Never take a woman for granted."

"Say, what *is* this?" His lips thinned. "Could the busy social schedule be due to Grant Stevenson?"

"I'm having dinner with him if that's what you mean. For heaven's sake, Toby—stop acting like a wounded water buffalo. Grant just wants to eat dinner and learn about Sea Bend." She pulled up abruptly and asked, "By the way, when is the garbage collection at the cottage?"

"The what?" He stared at her as if she'd taken complete leave of her senses. "How the hell do I know?"

"Never mind."

He opened the door of his sports car with a jerk. "I don't know what's come over you, Jean. Maybe you didn't get enough sleep last night." He slid behind the wheel and slammed the door hard. "You're acting as if you're functioning on about four cylinders this morning. I'll probably see you at the Inn tonight unless your friend Grant plans to drive thirty miles up the coast to the next decent restaurant."

"I imagine we'll be at the Inn. Let me know if you

45

hear anything else about the plant, will you. I'm at the bottom of our superintendent's calling list."

"That's because he thinks women should stay in their proper place." Toby gunned his engine impatiently. "After talking to you this morning, I'm beginning to believe he's right."

She stepped back from the car. "And a good morning to you too."

He grinned unwillingly and gave her a brief salute before easing down the curving drive.

Jean put their coffee things on the tray and carried them back into the house.

Mrs. Lloyd came into the kitchen while she was rinsing them at the sink. "Leave those, Miss Jean— I'm almost finished with the dusting. Will Mr. Calhoun be here for lunch?"

" 'Fraid not . . . he's on his way to the golf course." She looked at her watch. "You'd better not count on me, either. I'll be late at the hospital if I don't get going."

"But what about your food?"

"Heavens, I just finished breakfast." She leaned over and dropped an impulsive kiss on the older woman's cheek. "You'll have me fifty pounds overweight if I don't watch out."

"That'll be the day. Do you want me to leave anything for your dinner?"

"No thanks, I've been invited out." She paused by the kitchen door. "You can start looking up recipes though. Mr. Winthrop's due soon and you know how he hates eating in restaurants."

Mrs. Lloyd nodded. "He doesn't even like staying at the Inn. Maybe it's just as well you only have one guest room. Otherwise he'd be staying here every time he came up to check on the operation of the plant." She sniffed audibly. "I suppose now he'll be all upset about that fire."

"How on earth did you hear about it?"

"That's stale news by now. They were talking about it at the bus terminal when I walked by this morning."

"I don't know why the government bothers with the

communications satellite," Jean said in admiration as she picked up a cardigan from a bench in the front hall.

"Aren't you going to change?" the other asked.

"I have two extra uniforms in the volunteers' lounge, so I'll do it there. See you tomorrow."

"All right. Don't forget to eat . . . d'ya hear?"

"I promise."

Mrs. Lloyd closed the door behind Jean and went to retrieve her vacuum. "All this big house," she muttered, "and that girl rattling around in it like a lost soul. Not eatin' enough to keep a gull flying and on the go so she won't have to sit around here and be lonesome."

She glanced thoughtfully at the long living room with its expanse of thermo-pane windows extending from floor to ceiling on the ocean side and mellow pecan paneling covering the other walls. A down davenport and chairs upholstered in rust and green accent colors complemented the honey shade of the paneling while the deeper green carpet provided a muted elegance to the surroundings.

"Not much good to own some place like this," the older woman went on, "when you have to live in it all by yourself. Toby Calhoun better get moving and change things around." She flicked the switch on the upright handle of the vacuum and a satisfying whirr filled the room, but she still stood there frowning down at it. The way Toby had lit off like a frightened pup didn't look too promising. What was it Ernie had said yesterday about Jean walking down the beach toward that cottage? If you put his remark together with Rick's report on the new tenant Grant Stevenson —Mrs. Lloyd gave the vacuum an energetic push and she hummed along with the noise of the motor. It might be a good thing if she ordered a little more wood and heard exactly what else Ernie had to say!

When Jean returned home late that afternoon, she noticed that Mrs. Lloyd's car was gone from its accustomed place by the garage and felt a surge of relief. While there was certainly nothing clandestine

47

about her dinner date with Grant, she preferred not to provide more grist for Sea Bend's gossip mill.

This way, her thoughts could be fully occupied with important things like deciding what dress to wear for the evening! Sea Bend residents were reluctant to discard their casual attire, but dinner at the Inn counted as a special occasion even for them. If she knew what Grant was wearing, it would be easier.

Finally she decided to compromise on a fine wool dress in teal blue. The cut was deceivingly simple, but a satin ruff of a collar in the same shade added a stylish fillip. Before she decided on a coat, she'd wait and see whether Grant was wearing a dark suit or something more casual. She was just slipping on a pair of brown pumps when she saw her paperboy pushing his bike up the drive to the house. Shoving up her bedroom window, she leaned out and hailed him.

"Hi Rick! You're out late."

He stopped and grinned up at her. "It's collecting night."

"So that's why I'm getting such service! Just a minute—I'll find some money and meet you at the front door." She pulled her head in and locked the window before taking her purse from the dressing table and hurrying out to meet him. Halfway to the front door, she paused and then detoured through the kitchen for a handful of sugar cookies. Wrapping them in a napkin, she went on out to the front hall and swung open the door.

Rick was sitting on the lower step laboriously making out a receipt. His tongue protruded slightly as he filled in facts and figures.

Jean dropped the package of cookies in his lap. "That's hungry work, Rick. These will keep your strength up until you get home."

"Gee thanks, Miss Cameron. How did ya know?"

"If I had to get a bicycle up that drive, I'd need more than cookies," she admitted, opening her wallet. She watched him accept her money and carefully tear out the receipt.

Once business formalities were completed, his behavior reverted to normal. "You're all dressed up," he noted. "Are you going to have company?"

"Sort of. Thanks for the kind words."

"Is Mr. Winthrop coming to see you?"

Jean raised her eyebrows. "Why do you ask that?"

"I saw him driving down Main street a little while ago."

A flicker of annoyance passed over her face. So Bart was already in town—it was a wonder he hadn't telephoned to announce his arrival. What a blessing that she would be unavailable for a few more hours thanks to Grant.

"He'll probably be around." She watched him consume a cookie. "I hope those don't spoil your dinner. Speaking of dinner, won't your mother be worried if you don't get home pretty soon?"

Rick displayed total unconcern. "She knows where I am. Besides, I'm late because she wouldn't let me start collecting this afternoon until I took care of Maximilian."

"What's wrong with that iguana now?"

"He had a carrot stuck on his tooth and it made Mom sort of upset."

"With Maximilian?"

He nodded. "I told her Max didn't care whether he had a carrot stuck on his tooth or not. He looked sort of funny with it sticking out the side of his mouth, but she kept saying I had to get it off." He reached for another cookie. "I s'pose it was my fault for letting him out of his cage in the first place. Mom's not keen on finding him in the kitchen."

"Women are like that," she said diplomatically.

"I guess so. Anyway, Max finally rubbed the carrot off when he hid behind the stove. I had to get him back in his cage so Mom could come down off the chair. Our house isn't really the proper atmosphere for Max, I guess." He looked up hopefully. "You're sure that you don't . . ."

"Positive!" Then to make doubly sure: "The open fireplaces around here would be terrible hazards for an iguana."

"I suppose you're right." Rick wasn't really convinced.

Fortunately their conversation was interrupted by the sound of a car coming up the drive.

"Your company's come," Rick announced. Then, glimpsing a sleek black car, "Hey! That's Mr. Stevenson's Thunderbird." He bounced up from the front step still clutching two cookies and dashed over to where Grant was pulling up by the corner of the patio. "Hi, Mr. Stevenson! Bet 'cha didn't guess you'd be seeing me again so soon."

"I certainly didn't." Grant unfolded his long legs and stepped out onto the gravel. "If you'd told me we were calling on the same lady, I'd have given you a lift." His whimsical gaze moved over to acknowledge Jean's presence. For an instant, whimsy changed to something else and then his attention was back on Rick.

"Heck, I'm not calling," the youngster was saying. "I'm collecting. Just like at your house."

"Except that at mine, you inquired after Homer's well-being." He translated for Jean's benefit: "Homer is in excellent health but Rick thinks he's a trifle lonesome."

"I could get him a friend. . . ." Rick started.

"But I told him that Homer and I were company for each other. Plenty of company for each other," Grant finished firmly.

"I see you have the measure of the man," Jean agreed. "More cookies, Rick?"

"No thanks, Miss Cameron. I'd better get going. It's almost time to fix Max's dinner and I want to get to the hamburger before my mom does. It's easier than flies," he added cryptically.

Jean shuddered. "I should think so."

He strolled over to his bike. "See you tomorrow."

"See you," Jean confirmed.

"So long, Rick," Grant said.

The paperboy threw a leg over his bike and was off down the drive.

Jean turned to find Grant surveying the two sunken

garbage cans by her garage door. "Don't get any ideas," she warned.

"What an attitude! Here I am without any . . . and you . . ."

"Have the normal number and intend to keep them, thank you. Besides, I talked to Toby's secretary today and she said she had already solved your problem, so you can stop acting like a forsaken man." She gave him a quick glance, noting the conventional dark suit and liking what she saw. Tonight he looked more like a rising stockbroker than an artist. "I just have to get a coat," she said hastily as she intercepted a quizzical stare. "Would you like to come in for a drink?"

He glanced at his watch. "There isn't time if we make our dinner reservation. It was a case of very early or very late and frankly—I'm starved."

"So am I. . . . I won't be a minute." She went back into the hall and took her silk topcoat from the closet. Grant's dark suit was a nice change from Toby's casual attire. It practically took a wedding or a funeral to part him from a sport coat. She paused to check the contents of her purse and then went back outside. "I'm ready."

Grant whistled softly as he opened the car door for her. "Very nice too! I knew that makeshift outfit didn't do you justice last night, but I didn't realize there'd be *that* much difference."

"There was tremendous room for improvement," she said noncommittally, wondering whether he was referring to corduroy trousers or the green silk dressing gown. She watched him tuck her skirt carefully aside before he closed the heavy door and went around to the driver's side. Evidently he had no intention of explaining.

As soon as he edged the car down the drive he said casually, "There's a beautiful view from up here."

She smiled politely, taking her cue from him. "Wonderful . . . at all seasons. During the winter, the surf looks like a witch's cauldron and in the summer the sunsets are fabulous."

"There's enough room on the estate to build five or

51

six houses. It's no wonder Toby Calhoun has his eye on it."

"How on earth did you hear about that?"

He slanted a grin at her before turning back to concentrate on the road ahead. "You're one of Sea Bend's favorite topics. It isn't every day they get an heiress in their midst."

"I told you not to believe all you hear. Remember, I can't sell the property unless I get married."

"It's too bad your uncle didn't have more faith in women." Then, shrugging, "Oh well, the probate can't take forever and it sounds like an inheritance worth waiting for."

"I know."

"Has Toby heard about the marriage clause?"

"We've never discussed it, but the Calhouns aren't worrying about where their next meal is coming from."

"So I understand." He braked before easing out onto the main road and then accelerated. "Incidentally, I got in touch with Ernie this morning and told him to keep quiet about seeing you at the cottage."

Jean felt a warmth go over her cheeks. "That was thoughtful of you. If he started spreading rumors, I really would be in trouble."

"I don't understand."

"It's another part of the darned will. My uncle didn't have too much faith in feminine morals either. He had an unhappy love affair years ago and his fiancée ran off with another man. Anyhow—to get to the point—during the time I'm living in Sea Bend, my actions have to be above reproach. If the executor gets wind of anything else, he could make it difficult." She smiled grimly. "I heard that he arrived in town this afternoon, so it's just as well you assured Ernie I wasn't living in sin last night."

"Damn! You should have said something."

"Why? Other than your carrying me piggyback all the way up the beach, there wasn't a thing we could do about it." She surveyed her ankle with a frown. "Who would ever believe a story about a sprained ankle?"

52

He glanced down at it. "It looks fine now."

"It is," she sighed. "All it needed was some rest."

Grant pulled up at the street's only traffic light opposite the statue of an intrepid pioneer, who stared at them with a morose expression. His weary stance indicated that he was thoroughly sick and tired of pointing a bronze finger ever westward.

"Sea Bend's claim to culture," Jean informed Grant. "He reminds me of a theater usher telling you the only seats are down front."

"Peasant! Anybody could see he's trying to hail a cab in the rain." A horn honked behind them and Grant glanced up at the green traffic light, swore softly and accelerated with a swiftness that made Jean catch her breath. "Sorry." He eased off. "You and your statues! I should have been watching what I was doing."

It was just a few more blocks until they turned off on a steep road which led directly to the Inn. The rambling cedar structure was built in the style of an Indian long house and Grant stopped by the heavily carved door to turn the car over to a parking attendant.

"Looks as if they're doing well tonight," he said, joining Jean by the entrance. "I thought this was the off-season."

"It is, but lots of people prefer the beach during the stormy months. Ernie tells me the Inn is booked solidly throughout the year."

Grant grinned as he put his shoulder to the massive door. "Well, Ernie should know."

Once inside, the rugged "outdoors" motif stopped. A deep-piled carpet with a discreet Indian pattern led down three steps toward a dimly lit bar at one end of the room and a luxurious dining area at the other. The glassed-in cooking area in the center spotlighted Indian chefs cooking salmon steaks over open alder wood fires. Primitive tribal wood-carvings were accorded places of honor on the walls and a gigantic thunderbird decorated the table where the *maître d'hôtel* was checking his reservations.

53

He nodded pleasantly. "Good evening Miss Cameron . . . Mr. Stevenson. Would you like to go right to your table?"

Grant consulted his watch. "Give us a few minutes in the bar first, will you?"

"Certainly, sir. The table will be ready when you want to order."

"Fine, thanks." Grant gestured for Jean to precede him toward the subdued lighting of the bar. "I'm not going to miss out on collecting that drink you owe me."

She wrinkled her nose as she glanced up at him. "I was afraid of that. There goes my budget unless you'd like lemonade. Ernie mixes a very good one."

"Not a chance," he said as they sat down in a quiet corner. "Speaking of Ernie, I see him beaming at us. I think we're going to get personal service."

Jean looked over to see Ernie's white-jacketed figure striding toward them. "I wonder why? Hi Ernie!" she greeted him, "how are you tonight?"

"Fine, Jean. Evening, Mr. Stevenson. I saw your name on the reservation list. Special occasion?"

"You bet—the lady's buying."

Jean cut in. "That's my cue to ask for some of your nicest champagne."

Grant's lips twitched. "I knew I picked the right partner last night."

She flushed at Ernie's sudden grin. He shook his head reassuringly.

"Mr. Stevenson told me all about that. You needn't have worried, Jean. Mr. Winthrop won't get anything out of me."

"Winthrop?" Grant asked, frowning.

"Yeah . . . Bart Winthrop," Ernie supplied. "I hear he's in town. I'll get that champagne for you." He hurried back to the bar.

Jean slipped out of her coat and shrugged it around her shoulders with Grant's help. "Bart's the executor I was telling you about."

"There's an industrialist with that name in Los Angeles. Any connection?"

"If you mean the Bart Winthrop who's in plastics

54

and electronics—it's the same one." She turned to look at him more directly. "Do you know him?"

He rubbed the side of his nose reflectively. "Slightly. Remember that young lady I was telling you about last night—the one who's getting the serious ideas?"

"The reason behind our mutual benefit pact?"

"That's the one. She's . . ."

"Here you are," Ernie interrupted as he deposited a silver wine bucket by their side and put two champagne glasses on the table in front of them. "Best in the house. Nothing's too good for an occasion like this."

"In that case, get another glass," Jean told him laughing.

"I accept . . . we're not too busy this early." He glanced over toward the bar. "I want to show you a cake my wife decorated. The manager says she's getting good enough to handle some of the special orders here."

"I'd like to see it," Jean assured him. As he disappeared into a nearby storage room, she explained to Grant. "Ernie's wife just finished a special course in cake decorating. If she can earn some money on the side, then he could stop working at so many odd jobs. They have a lot of medical bills to pay."

"Sounds like a good solution."

"When Ernie interrupted, you were telling about your friend." She kept her voice light with an effort. "Surely she isn't connected with my executor?"

He nodded grimly. "Her uncle. Hasn't he mentioned Doreen?"

Jean straightened as if she'd swallowed a poker. "I had no idea that you meant her."

"Here it is," Ernie said, placing an elaborately decorated three-layer wedding cake in front of them. "How about that for a beautiful job!"

"Ernie—it's gorgeous!" Jean's voice was distracted but her admiration was sincere. "It's a really professional job."

"Yeah," his grin stretched from ear to ear. "My boss thought we should keep a couple cakes in the freezer all the time for unexpected bridal parties." He was deftly easing the cork from their wine bottle as he spoke and the sudden pop as it erupted penetrated the conversational hum.

"You forgot to get a glass for yourself," Grant reminded Ernie.

"I'll take care of that right away." He filled their glasses carefully. "Be back in a minute."

"In the meantime . . ." Grant raised his glass to Jean, "to our pact."

She touched his glass lightly in response. Suddenly she was conscious that the pianist in the corner of the room had switched from a nostalgic ballad to an elaborately arranged rendition of *Lohengrin*. Puzzled, she looked around to see the bridal couple and became aware that the raised glasses and soft applause from the occupants of the room were directed squarely at her. She set her glass down so hard on the table that some of the contents spilled on the polished wood.

"Good heavens, Grant—they think . . ." She was interrupted by a shrill feminine voice at her elbow.

"Grant! What in the world's going on?" The words came from a petite redhead elegantly dressed in navy blue chiffon, but the stentorian tone was worthy of a Wagnerian soprano.

"Doreen!" Grant shot to his feet like a rocket being launched.

"I'd like an answer too, Jean."

Jean's panicky gaze focused on the gray-haired man standing behind his irate niece. His heavy-lidded eyes narrowed as they took in the table full of champagne and wedding cake.

"Bart!" The word came out in a gulp. "I heard you were in town. Have you met Grant? We were just celebrating . . ." Her inane attempt at conversation stopped abruptly as she tried to stifle a sudden panic at the expression on his face.

"So I see. Too bad you didn't see fit to invite me to the wedding, or don't executors rate an announcement?"

At that moment, Ernie, carrying an empty champagne glass, arrived and surveyed the situation. "Well,

I'll be damned! You promised me yesterday I'd be the *first* to know," he complained, wrapping a muscular arm around Jean's shoulders and hugging her. "And that husband of yours was telling me to keep mum about having you in his cabin at five o'clock this morning."

Jean decided the sudden roaring in her ears was caused by the walls tumbling down around her. On the other side of the table, Grant stood like a marble statue.

"Who were you trying to kid?" Ernie continued. He turned and shouted to another bartender. "Hey Fred —bring some more glasses."

"By all means." Sarcasm dripped from Doreen Winthrop's voice. "We must celebrate this happy occasion. May we sit down, Grant?" The venom in her look would have stopped a charging rhino in his tracks.

"Of course." His words came out slowly. "Let me help you with that chair." He had all the enthusiasm of a nine-year-old at dancing class.

"Thank you." She subsided gracefully while her uncle made an imperative gesture for another chair to be brought for him. "Now darling," she continued, "introduce me to your wife."

There was a moment of strained silence while Grant looked grimly over at Jean. She clenched her fingers in her lap and was scarcely aware of the pain as her nails cut into her palms. In the corner of the room, the pianist had switched playfully into Gilbert and Sullivan's "Make the Punishment Fit the Crime."

Finally Grant spoke. "Jean . . . may I present Doreen Winthrop."

Jean nodded jerkily as if her head might part company from her shoulders at any moment.

"Doreen. . . . this is Jean. . . ." Grant's voice trailed off dismally at the moment of truth.

The redhead reached out to the wedding cake on the table in front of them and plucked off a white sugar rose, which she deliberately pulverized between her slender fingers. Only after she had blown the crumbs from her hand did she acknowledge the introduction.

"Jean Cameron Stevenson," she said balefully. "You could have told us, Grant . . . or was it such a hurried affair that you couldn't invite your friends?"

"What's the difference?" Ernie plunged into the awkward silence that followed Doreen's words. "We're all here to celebrate at the reception. I'll get some more glasses and a knife to cut the cake. This is a real occasion."

"So was Waterloo and now I know just how Napoleon felt," Doreen informed him bitterly. "Never mind—bring some more champagne. It should come in handy—one way or another."

Chapter FOUR

Despite Ernie's fond hopes, the evening was not an unqualified success.

Doreen simmered with anger, Grant relapsed into long periods of silence, Bart was an offended senior citizen, and Jean had a tendency to jump when the waiter dropped a spoon. Midway through dinner, Toby appeared to provide the finishing touch.

His reaction on hearing the matrimonial news was just what Jean had feared. After a violent initial reaction, he proceeded to sulk in offended silence for the rest of the evening while rapidly consuming double Scotches.

As time went by, Grant's morose expression deepened—giving the impression that he had attended more festive wakes in his time. Jean eyed him nervously and wished that she could run screaming to the nearest exit. Anything to get away from the accusing glances surrounding her; any place to sort out her confused thoughts.

But it appeared that solitude was not to be had—even at the end of that long evening.

"I tried to phone you," Bart told her austerely as he brushed cigar ashes from his lapel. "Since we arrived a day early, the Inn can't honor my reservation until tomorrow." He waited expectantly.

"I only have one extra bedroom . . ."

"I realize that. Naturally I had no idea that we would be imposing on a honeymoon couple. . . ."

"We?" she squeaked.

"Doreen needs a room too," he said flatly. "You'll have to make some sort of arrangements."

Toby looked up from his drink long enough to mumble, "No trouble 'bout that. You can stay in Stevenson's cabin and Doreen stays with the newly-weds." He peered at them owlishly. "Must be dishcreet and not disturb the con . . . connubyul bliss."

Grant opened his mouth, but Doreen spoke first.

"What a dandy idea!"

Grant closed his mouth again, but gave Toby a look which obviously consigned him to the lions.

"Isn't it, darling?" Doreen was insistent.

"It's Jean's house," Grant said finally.

And I'd sooner have a tiger with a sore paw, thought Jean. Aloud, she said, "Of course, we'd love to have you. It should all work out very well." There was no doubt about it—she was developing a positive talent for lying in her teeth. She sighed and picked up her coat.

"Are we going now?" Doreen asked.

"If you don't mind. I should get home and prepare your room."

"Don't forget—these people are still at the stage where they prefer a little privacy," Bart announced with a heavy attempt at humor. "I'm surprised they left home."

"So am I," Jean improvised brightly. "This whole evening has been a revelation."

"One of the joys of marriage," Grant told her. "You'll get used to them in time."

"I'm sure I will . . . now I've survived the initial shock."

His look was sardonic. "And think of all that's yet to come."

"I am," she said defiantly. "That's why I get this ringing in my ears."

"Sounds like low blood pressure to me," Doreen observed.

"I do *not* have low blood pressure."

"Well, it's not a very bridelike thing to say," the other said suspiciously.

"But then Jean's not a conventional bride," Grant said. "Ours is a special case. Isn't it, darling?"

"That's for sure."

"You're supposed to smile when you say that," he told her gravely.

"I don't want to hear any more," Toby said, lurching to his feet. "I'm goin' home." His lower lip drooped. "Thish been a hell of a night."

"You're in no condition to drive," Jean began.

"Don't worry," Bart interrupted, "I'll give Toby a lift. I'll need your key to the cottage, Grant."

The other handed it over. "Make yourself at home."

"Oh, I plan to." Bart jammed his cigar butt into an ashtray with some force. "We'd better arrange a time for you to come over to the plant tomorrow afternoon. There will be some papers for you to sign now that you're a member of the family." He stood up, his hand resting negligently on the chair back. "Strange how things happen, isn't it? I was offering you a job a few weeks ago and now you're coming into the plant up here as a major stockholder."

Grant's only outward reaction was a slight thinning of his lips.

Bart went on. "That Horatio Alger story should be changed to 'go north young man.' Maybe I underestimated you, Grant."

"I thought I was goin' home," Toby put in querulously.

"We are, my boy." Bart turned with authority. "Doreen—I'll leave your luggage with the bell captain. See you all tomorrow."

Toby's muttered good night was directed at the floor and his dignified exit seemed a triumph of self-control.

"We're next, I guess," Doreen said, getting up. "I want to check that luggage transfer myself. I'll meet you both out at the car."

Jean watched her graceful exit and then turned to see Grant leaving a bill on the table for a tip.

"Ready?" he asked briefly.

"I suppose so." She paused and then burst out, "You mean, that's all you have to say at a time like this?"

"I'm perfectly ready to have a sane discussion—in a low tone of voice," he said pointedly, "whenever we have a little privacy. I certainly don't intend to do it with half the residents of Sea Bend looking on." He pushed back his chair and stood up. "Shall we go?"

"By all means," Jean said through clenched teeth. "Shall we make an appointment later this week? The way things are going, I can't see a free moment before. Maybe by then, you can tell me why we're in this farce."

He grasped her elbow to help her up the steps and from his expression she had the feeling he would have preferred a grip on her throat. His next words confirmed it.

"I wish to God I knew. Ernie's bright confession about your overnight stay didn't help. What the devil was I supposed to say?"

Jean rubbed her forehead wearily. "I don't know. Ask Doreen. She has the answer for everything."

"Don't underestimate her."

"Underestimate her? Not a chance. I'd rather have a hungry cobra for a house guest."

"Calm down, for pete's sake," he said severely as they paused on the front steps and waited for the car. "Things are going to be tough enough without your behaving like that."

"I'll try to restrain myself, but when we have that minute you can tell me why Bart offered you a job a few weeks ago. What did he want with an artist?"

Grant watched the parking attendant switch on the lights of the Thunderbird and avoided her upturned gaze. "I told you I'd explain later," he said.

"I hope it's a good story. . . ."

"Anyone would think we *were* married—the way you're going on."

"Thanks a heap."

The long black car was braked with a flourish in front of them. Jean surveyed the cozy bucket seats in front before saying with determination, "I'll sit in the back."

"There's no need. . . ."

She shook off Grant's restraining hand and climbed into the rear seat. "It will help me remember my place."

Doreen's arrival effectively stopped further discussion, but the grim look on Grant's face gave warning that it was merely postponed rather than canceled.

Bart's niece settled herself gracefully in front as if she were expecting such courtesy. "I asked the boy to put all my bags in the trunk." She peered up at Grant. "Was that all right, darling?"

"Sure." He glanced at the formidable pile. "Never let it be said that you travel light."

"You should know, sweetie. Remember when we spent that weekend at Palm Desert? You said I'd brought enough luggage to go straight to Zamboanga."

There was an audible sniff from the back seat. Grant glared that way before slamming his car door violently and starting the engine with a roar.

Doreen squeaked in protest as they took off like an entry in the *Grand Prix*. "Grant! Do you always drive like this?"

"You should know, sweetie," he mimicked bitterly.

That took care of the conversation until they pulled up in front of Jean's house a little later.

"I'll go ahead and turn on the lights," Jean said to Doreen. "You can tell Grant what bags you'll need for tonight."

For the first time, Doreen looked nonplused. "Well, actually I might have to stay a little longer than overnight."

Grant turned off the ignition. "I thought Bart said that his reservation at the Inn was for tomorrow."

"*His* reservation is," the other admitted. "I just de-

63

cided to come along on the spur of the moment, so I didn't bother to arrange for a room ahead of time." She looked up defiantly. "How on earth was I to know that they're booked with a convention all week?"

Jean stifled a sigh and decided there was no use in losing her temper again. There was also no use suggesting that Doreen try a motel in the next town. After the mix-up earlier in the evening, she was in no position to arouse Bart's suspicions still further. Grant's grim expression proved that he wasn't thrilled by the circumstances either. Probably it was just as well Doreen was on hand for propriety's sake until the situation was resolved.

Grant cleared his throat suggestively as he unloaded the first two pieces of luggage from the trunk.

Jean hastily interrupted her reverie to unlock the front door and turn on the lights. "You'd better put Doreen's things in the guest room," she told him. Then, catching the frown that passed over his face, she said hurriedly, "I'll go ahead and see if everything's ready." She added in a low tone for his ears alone, "Sorry—I forgot that you weren't familiar with the house."

His only response was a noncommittal grunt. She led the way down the main hall and then turned left into a spacious twin bed room decorated in soft grays and blues.

"This is very nice," Doreen admitted, putting an expensive-looking leather tote bag down on a needlepoint luggage rack. "Uncle Bart didn't tell me how elegant it was."

"I hope you'll be comfortable." Jean waved toward the open doorway on her left. "Your bath's adjoining. My room . . ." She caught herself and said instead, "The master bedroom is just across the hall."

"I'm surprised your uncle didn't build on." Doreen smoothed an eyebrow as she glanced at the mirror over the dressing table. "Just two bedrooms . . . in a location like this!"

"He liked it this way," Jean said defensively, "and I've had no reason to change."

The redhead looked over her shoulder at Grant, who was lounging in the hall doorway. "What are your plans, Grant? I thought you were the sociable type."

He shrugged. "The only thing I'm planning right now is getting some sleep."

"Spoken like a true gentleman. All right—I can take a hint." Doreen threw her purse onto a bedspread with unnecessary force. "Don't let me disturb you."

"You won't," Jean replied, not quite truthfully. "The housekeeper usually comes in to serve breakfast around eight."

"Thanks—but I never bother with breakfast. I'll see you at lunch," Doreen said definitely.

"Whatever you'd like. Coffee's available any time in case you change your mind." Jean paused by the door. "I hope you sleep well."

"Thanks." Doreen's voice was muffled as she bent over a piece of luggage. "Good night."

Grant silently trailed Jean into the master bedroom and watched her hang her coat in the closet. His glance took in the oversize double bed, but his only reaction was to perch on the arm of a yellow chair and flip through the pages of a paperback left on its cushion as if he had all the time in the world.

He might at least have the decency to look up, Jean decided, as she needlessly straightened the porcelain mirror above her dressing table.

Grant's next utterance proved that he was on the same track even if his attention was supposedly focused on her reading material. "I suppose," he said grimly, "that we'll have to play out this farce for the rest of the night."

"Umm."

He did glance up then as if suddenly aware of her silence. "Cheer up! There's no need to look like the family ghost. We'd better stop sniping and get back to our mutual assistance pact."

"All right." She ran her fingers through her hair and kneaded the area around her temples. "I'll function better after a couple of aspirin. Somewhere along the line, I've collected a dilly of a headache."

"A cup of coffee should help. Let's go out to the kitchen and make some," he said, standing up.

"But coffee will keep you awake," she protested automatically.

His amused gaze swept the room with its solitary bed. "Is that bad?"

"No—I see what you mean."

He held up a warning hand as she started for the door. "Be quiet, for lord's sake. I could do without Doreen for the rest of the night." He went on as he caught sight of her surprised expression. "I might as well set the record straight on one thing. That weekend in Palm Desert was adequately chaperoned and perfectly proper . . . believe it or not."

"I'll believe it." For the first time in hours, Jean felt life had some redeeming qualities. "What does Amy Vanderbilt suggest for our situation?"

"I don't know, but the groom suggests coffee. You'd better give me a quick tour of the house on the way. That will save me from leading Bart into the linen closet when he suggests going out onto the patio."

She nodded. "I'll give you an extra house key too. I can see where we need that coffee—this is going to be complicated." Later, as they sat hunched over the kitchen table, she suggested half-seriously, "Maybe we should leave tonight. You could go to Mexico and I could try Canada for a few weeks."

He put his coffee cup in the saucer decisively. "Thanks but no thanks."

"Artists have a wonderful time in Mexico."

"Where did you get the idea that I was Picasso's successor? My only talent in that line runs to restaining patio chairs."

"Rick must have started the wrong rumor." Her look was searching. "I didn't think you seemed the type."

"I'm not sure whether that's a compliment or not."

"Pay no attention to any comments I make at this time of night." She stirred her coffee aimlessly. "What kind of a job did Bart try to hire you for?"

"I'm a chemical engineer for his strongest competitor down in Los Angeles."

"Did Doreen have anything to do with his job offer?"

That glacial look came back into his eyes. "I haven't needed a woman's help to get a job yet."

"Ouch!" She made an apologetic grimace. "Sorry—she does have a pretty possessive attitude."

"She had that on our first date. Unfortunately she also has the determination of a Sherman tank. That's why I enlisted your help in the first place."

Jean's smile was crooked. "Lo, what a tangled web we weave. . . ."

He shrugged. "What else could we do? It was common knowledge that we spent last night at the cottage. You'd just told me that as your executor Bart could have used that knowledge to make things difficult for you." His eyebrows drew together suddenly. "Did you get the impression that he wasn't exactly delighted with our glad tidings?"

"Bart wants control of the plywood company," she said flatly. "Now he thinks he'll have to deal with you as well. A chemical engineer will be more trouble than a woman who scarcely knows one part of the process from another."

"Possibly." He shoved his chair back and stood up to prowl around the kitchen. "I do know that we've gotten so impossibly deep in this situation that we'll have to go through with it."

"What do you mean?" Her whispered query barely carried to where he was leaning against the sink.

"Merely that we have to make the whole thing legal." He shoved his hands deep in his pockets. "Bart wants me to start signing estate documents tomorrow afternoon. From then on, the charade becomes reality."

"You could always go back to California on the first plane," she suggested unhappily.

"There you go again." He shook his head. "Don't you realize that Bart would call my boss first thing to find out why his lab chief had deserted his bride. The

67

next move would be to swear out a warrant—he could take his choice on charges."

"It doesn't sound good when you put it that way."

"Believe me—that's the way he'd put it. I know Bart's reputation. A temporary marriage is the only way out."

At his calm pronouncement, Jean's stomach lurched as if she'd boarded an express elevator. "How do you get married in a hurry?" she managed finally.

"I know a judge who's not too far away. I'm hoping he'll bend a few requirements since he's an old friend of the family. Even if he doesn't, I can't see why Bart would feel compelled to check the date on our marriage license. At any rate, I'll find out when I'm sure Doreen's asleep and can't overhear on her extension phone."

Jean shook her head without speaking and then got up to rummage in the cupboard for a bottle of aspirin.

"Still have your headache?" Grant asked sympathetically.

She nodded, then smiled wryly. "It must be bridal nerves. How are we supposed to manage the rest of the night?"

"That's up to you."

Her cheeks flamed and she marched back to swallow the aspirin with a sip of coffee. "I can recommend the couch in the living room," she said finally. "It should be as good as the one I used in the cottage."

"Use your head, woman. Bridegrooms don't spend honeymoon nights in the living room."

Jean's glance was withering. "*This* one does."

"Okay. You explain to Doreen when she wanders around in the middle of the night."

"Damn!" She drew in her breath sharply. "I forgot about Doreen."

"Well, I haven't."

"Wait a minute! We can bring in one of the lounges from the patio . . . they fold up completely and tomorrow I can hide it in my closet." She frowned in concentration. "You'll have to hand it up through the

68

bedroom window to me. It wouldn't do to have Doreen see you carry it down the hall."

"Okay. I guess that's the best we can do." He tried to interpret her expression. "Now what's wrong?"

She gestured toward his dark suit. "Permanent press is great, but even the manufacturers don't recommend sleeping in the garment."

"I'll try to duck down to the cottage and change tomorrow morning before anybody notices the wrinkles."

"You won't have to!" Her features had suddenly brightened. "I can even solve that. My housekeeper's church guild gave me some clothes for hospital emergency cases. You know, patients who haven't a chance to get their own things right away. I'm sure there was a robe and pajamas in the collection. . . ."

"At this point, I'm not fussy. How about blankets?"

"That's easy. There are some in the hall closet."

"Okay. You hunt out a blanket and my costume for tonight." He went over to the kitchen door. "I'll get one of the lounges and shove it through the window. Then you take first shift in the bathroom and leave the premises clear for me."

"You make it sound like a tactical battle plan," she protested.

"It is." He opened the door quietly. "And you can't afford to lose."

Once put into effect, Grant's schedule worked amazingly well. He assured Jean the pajamas she unearthed from the rummage pile were perfectly adequate even though they were mid-shin length. If he suspected that their former owner had passed to his heavenly reward, he remained discreetly silent and shrugged cheerfully into the matching blue robe.

"I hope that lounge is going to be long enough for you," Jean said, eyeing it doubtfully. "It might be better if we switched around and you took the bed."

"Don't be silly. This will be fine." He was transferring his cigarettes and lighter to the robe pocket.

"You'll fall off if you don't turn over carefully."

"At a height of six inches the results shouldn't be

69

fatal." He perched on the chair by the window. "You'd better go to bed. Do you mind if I have a cigarette before I turn in?"

"No . . . of course not." She sidled over to the bed and tried to decide how to get into it without looking nervous in the process. She was also regretting her choice of nightgown. Undressing earlier, she had concluded that her faded corduroy brunch coat was hardly suitable for the occasion. She had ruthlessly ignored the logic of this reasoning and merely reached for a particularly becoming black velour robe banded in a leopard print. The matching gown featured an opaque nylon jersey skirt but the bodice and sleeves were of whisper-thin chiffon. That the robe would come off while the light was still on was a disconcerting development.

Her fingers toyed nervously with the end of her belt as she hovered by the bed. Obviously she couldn't keep the robe on without appearing an utter fool.

Grant's amused voice cut through the silence. "If it makes you feel better, I'll turn discreetly toward the wall."

Annoyed that he had fathomed the reason for her dithering, she spun around to face him. "That wasn't the reason I was hesitating," she lied defiantly.

He calmly lit his cigarette. "No? Then I can relax and not have to stare pointedly out the window."

"Please yourself." She turned her back to him and in one fluid motion deposited her robe on the foot of the bed while sliding under the covers. Hauling the sheet safely up to her chin, she wriggled until both pillows were propped behind her. Only then did she look back at Grant.

He was stretched out and staring thoughtfully at the white brick fireplace on the far wall of the room. She needn't have worried about her filmy bodice at all.

For a split second, the memory of Doreen's possessive manner came back to haunt her. Perhaps Grant had protested too much. The memory of that beautiful redhead must have been potent for any man.

"You're looking remarkably wide awake for this

time of night." Grant observed her casually. "Want me to turn out that light on your bed table?"

"No thanks—I like it." She wished he wouldn't take that elder brother tone each time he addressed her.

"Shining in your eyes?"

"Always." She punched a pillow balefully. "Don't worry. I'll turn it out when you're ready for bed."

He stirred and stubbed out his cigarette. "I'm not worrying." He reached absently for another and then tossed the pack on the table without removing one.

"I suppose I shouldn't have had all that coffee," she said finally when the silence dragged on. "Now I'm not sleepy." She sat upright. "We could play gin rummy. There's a deck of cards in the drawer of the bed table and we can use the comforter for the discard pile."

Grant approached the bed slowly. His glance traveled down from her attractively tousled hair, past her questioning eyes to take in the lovely figure revealed by the sheer chiffon. Then, deliberately, he leaned over and turned off the lamp. "We are *not* playing gin rummy," he said.

The room was bathed solely in the moonlight filtering through the filmy curtains. He paused with his hand on the hall door. "I'm going out to the living room to read a dull book for a half hour."

"What about Doreen?" she protested.

"The hell with Doreen! Lie down and go to sleep."

"But I'm not sleepy."

"That's too damned bad!" Grant had obviously reached the end of his tether. "I'm not sleepy either and don't tell me I drank too much coffee." His hand tightened on the door knob. "Unless you really want to complicate this impossible situation, you'd better start counting sheep. That way you won't come up with any more thin-skulled ideas." He gave a last baleful look at her motionless figure. "Gin rummy! My God—that will be the day!"

Chapter *FIVE*

———◆———

There was a persistent tattoo playing on Jean's ears and groggily she pulled her pillow closer to shut it out. The wave of noise abated and she smiled gently, drifting back into a pleasant doze.

"Aren't you *ever* going to wake up? I've been pounding on that door forever!"

This time the interruption penetrated abruptly. Jean's eyes flew open and she hastily pushed up onto an elbow.

"Don't look so stricken." Doreen approached the bedside carrying a glass of orange juice in one hand and a steaming mug of coffee in the other. "I've come bearing gifts and instructed to say my apologies nicely." She looked as if she'd been up for hours and her light makeup was as immaculate as her white Italian silk shift with outsize daisy appliqués on the hem.

Jean blinked in confusion. "How nice of you." Her voice sounded stilted to her own ears and she struggled to sit up straighter. "I didn't expect such service." As memory came flooding back, she sent a horror-stricken glance toward the floor, but the lounge and blankets had been spirited from view.

"I told Grant that you'd probably send me packing

but I'd try." Doreen pushed aside the bed lamp and put the coffee mug down beside it. She offered the orange juice to Jean. "Try this—it's just out of the squeezer."

"Thanks." Jean took it gratefully. "Weren't you going to sleep in? What time is it?"

"Only eight o'clock but I couldn't sleep. Grant said it was probably my guilty conscience keeping me awake."

"Where is . . ." Jean broke off in the middle of her question. Brides shouldn't have to ask where their husbands were. She tried to assume a casual air. "Grant's an early bird too."

"I know," Doreen said complacently as she perched on the end of the bed. "I heard him out in the kitchen and decided to join him."

"For breakfast?"

"Of course. What else?"

"Sorry—I must be still half-asleep." It would help, Jean decided, if she knew where in the dickens Grant was. She put down the juice glass and swung her legs over the edge of the bed. "I should be out getting breakfast instead of having you two do all the work. Mrs. Lloyd . . ."

". . . Won't be in until later. She called a few minutes ago." Doreen straightened a daisy petal on her skirt. "There's no need for you to hurry. Grant won't be back to pick you up until ten. He said to tell you that he'd confirmed the appointment . . . whatever that means."

Jean turned to stare at her. "I didn't know he'd gone out."

"A few minutes ago. He told me that he had to feed Homer." Doreen frowned. "When did Grant start taking up with goldfish?"

"Just recently . . . he was a gift from a mutual friend," Jean said, taking a sip of her coffee. "Grant probably wanted to change clothes too. We'd been using his cottage," she added hurriedly.

"So he said. I didn't think he seemed very familiar with the kitchen." Doreen's downbent head muffled her

73

next words. "I'm sorry that I acted like such a spoiled brat last night but it was a shock. Matrimony was always the furthest thing from Grant's mind. At least that's the impression he gave to me all these months." Her smile was rueful. "Evidently I didn't have the right combination."

"These things happen," Jean put in lamely.

"So he said. I should have known he was the type to have a girl back home."

"Back home?" Jean's voice was faint. Where in the world *was* Grant's home town?

"Well . . . practically. He told how you'd known each other a long time ago and what a coincidence it was to meet again."

"Wasn't it!" Jean tried to infuse some enthusiasm into her tone. It would have been easier to play the part if Grant had given her a copy of the script first.

"And I can certainly see why you'd hurry up and get married before Uncle Bart caught wind of it."

"Oh? Why should he object?"

"Just on general principles." Doreen plucked at the comforter. "I'm sure he would rather have had Grant in his lab in Los Angeles. You know Uncle Bart—he isn't keen on taking in partners. He prefers employees. Anyway, that's his worry." She sat up and stretched like a graceful kitten. "Now that I've decided to behave myself—may I stay for a while? Grant said it was up to you." She added mischievously. "If I put it that way—you can't very well say no, can you?"

"Hardly."

"Even if it is scarcely polite to intrude on a person's honeymoon." Doreen wandered over to the dressing table, unstoppered a perfume bottle, and sniffed the fragrance appraisingly. "Umm, that's nice."

"Help yourself," Jean said, not quite sure which was the real Doreen—the unhappy woman of the previous night or the engaging creature in front of her.

"No thanks." The other replaced the stopper. "I'm not in favor of borrowing. Whether it's perfume or husbands."

Jean's lips twitched. "That's nice to know."

"Scout's honor. Now I'll go out and whip you up some breakfast as evidence of my good will."

"Keep it up and you'll be invited to stay for months." Jean paused with her hand on the dressing room door. "Don't worry about the cleaning up. Mrs. Lloyd sees to that."

"She won't have to bother today. Grant did most of the chores. He even took out the garbage."

"That's because those empty garbage cans fascinate him," Jean said absently.

"I beg your pardon?"

"Oh . . . nothing." She flushed under Doreen's mystified look and fled toward the bathroom saying, "Give me ten minutes."

Later in the shower, it occurred to her that most brides demanded more time to get ready on their wedding day and if Doreen had gotten Grant's message straight that's what he must have meant. Her fingers tensed on the mixing faucet as she thought it over. In a few hours, she'd be legally bound to a virtual stranger. Her lips quirked in a sad half-smile. If the same qualms were attacking Grant, it would be a wonder if he appeared at ten o'clock. No matter what, he'd probably be in a far worse mood than when he stormed out the bedroom door.

Preoccupied with her gloomy thoughts, she stepped under a cascade of icy water and was jerked back to reality. She gasped and hurriedly adjusted the spray. After all, there was no point in freezing. She sighed as she picked up the soap. Grant would probably manage the chilling process all by himself.

But when Grant did appear promptly at ten, his calm demeanor was in keeping with his impeccable appearance. The suit was light gray and he was wearing a white shirt with a subdued foulard tie. He looked immaculate and about as tractable as a weathered oak.

"Good morning," he said, gravely opening the car door for her.

"Good morning," she replied, wishing she could discipline her voice properly. "I didn't know what to wear. I hope this outfit is all right."

He surveyed her gold silk jacket dress impassively. "It looks very nice."

That banked-down response didn't do anything for her morale. She plunged on. "It's silly to be nervous, but I've never done anything like this before."

There was a poignant silence while her words dangled in midair.

And that, she thought frantically, must hold the record for inane remarks.

"Now that you mention it, neither have I," Grant said, giving her a strange look. "We didn't go into the question of discarded spouses, did we?"

"It wasn't necessary."

"I guess not." There was a trace of humor in his glance. "Just as well that we're a couple of innocents."

Innocents indeed! It was hard to imagine anyone more in control of a situation. She watched him go around the front of the car and decided it was high time to change the subject. "Doreen sent her best," she said as he turned the ignition key. "She called Toby and they took off on a golf date a half hour ago."

"Sounds as if she's planning to stay awhile." From the interest he was showing, they might have been discussing the trend of the commodity exchange.

She shifted to defensive tactics. "We mentioned it and I told her it was all right. Under the circumstances, it might be better to have another person in the house."

His lips tightened. "You're right, of course. Her testimony could come in handy when you apply for an annulment."

Jean stiffened perceptibly. "I wasn't thinking . . ."

"Do you ever?" he interrupted and then lifted an admonishing hand before she could flare in reply. "Sorry. That comment was ill-advised. This will work out all right."

She refused his olive branch. "I wish I shared your confidence. It looks like an unholy muddle to me." She paused and then went on without looking at him. "Obviously we'll have to make other sleeping arrangements. You can't exist on that lounge forever."

"I won't argue about that." He braked at the junction of the main road and turned onto the hard surface. "Now Bart's talking about staying at the cottage instead of the Inn, but I think I dissuaded him. We'll know for sure when we see him this afternoon."

"Are we going to have time to get . . . everything . . . done in time?"

"If you mean the wedding—yes."

"You needn't be stuffy about it. I do have an interest."

He smiled slightly. "All right, I'll climb down. The judge was obliging about waiving the waiting period. We're to meet him in his chambers at eleven-thirty. After the ceremony, we'll about have time for a hamburger before we drive back and meet Bart at the plant."

"What about the date on the license?"

"It will be today's date, but since we're out of Sea Bend there's no reason for anyone to question anything. The only newspaper is a weekly and we'll merely be a couple of strange names buried in the vital statistics column. The main thing is that our signatures will be legal for any documents this afternoon."

"It doesn't seem real," she protested.

"That's the best way to look at it. Remember that we were forced into a temporary state of affairs. Otherwise we'll end up really hating each other. If it makes you feel any better, you can cross your fingers when you say 'I do.'" He turned his head to give her an intent look and rested his hand lightly on her knee. "Friends, Jean?"

"Of course, Grant." She took a deep breath and wished she could break down and howl on his shoulder instead.

"Good." He patted her knee almost absently and put his hand back on the steering wheel.

Jean let a tiny sigh escape her as she risked a sideways glance at that rugged profile. There was no doubt about it; a stiff upper lip was the order of the day.

77

While their wedding ceremony wasn't a lavish affair, it was certainly the most discreet interlude possible. The judge greeted Grant as an old friend and her with old-world deference. The bare-bones ceremony was conducted with two of his staff as witnesses and was over in four minutes. They had signed the necessary papers and were on their way before Jean realized that she hadn't even been kissed. Grant needn't have made things *that* platonic, she thought bitterly.

"There's a place down here that makes pretty good hamburgers," he said as they pulled away from the curb in front of the courthouse. "I stopped there when I drove up from California." He let the car idle along in the slow lane of traffic. "Sound all right for lunch?"

"If you think there's time." The stiffness was back in her voice. After all, perfect strangers kissed each other on New Year's Eve. It wouldn't have killed him to make some kind of gesture.

"Well, do we?" he was asking.

"Do we what?"

"I was asking if we should break down and have them with onions," he said pulling up at a large drive-in on the corner. "It has to be a joint decision."

"Of course," she said brightly. "There's no reason not to. I always eat onions at wedding receptions."

There was a slight suspicious pause before he opened his window to give the order.

Jean withdrew in the far corner of her seat and stared with great interest at a rickety sign advertising bulk feed for cattle. Grant stared straight ahead and was evidently memorizing every price on the restaurant signboard. It was as if he had forgotten her very existence. When their order arrived, he managed to hand her a foil-wrapped burger without comment.

It was a good thing the drive-in didn't put cutlery on the tray, Jean decided. If there had been anything sharp within reach, she would have been tempted to kill the man.

The strained atmosphere persisted all the way back to Sea Bend. When the plant road came into sight, Grant turned off the highway without comment and pulled the car up in front of the ramshackle office annex which was an afterthought to the rambling sawmill and plywood sections beyond.

"Sorry sir, I'll have to ask you to move your car," said a uniformed plant guard coming up to Grant's window. "They're expecting some deliveries here today and we've been asked to keep this space clear."

"All right, officer. Where can I leave it?"

"I'll drive it behind the building for you if you like."

"Fine." He glanced at his watch. "We should go on in. Mr. Winthrop's expecting us."

Bart rose from behind a big mahogany desk to greet them when they entered the manager's office. "Right on time," he boomed genially. "I like punctual people."

"Where's Mr. Foster?" Jean asked looking around.

"I sent him into Portland to attend a meeting for me today. It's time he gets away from this place a little more. The manager of an operation this size should extend his personal horizons."

Jean looked at him skeptically. "I thought you believed in employees staying on the job."

"There's a time and a place for everything." He turned abruptly to Grant. "Has Jean shown you around the plant yet?"

"I haven't had a chance," she said, sitting on the arm of a leather chair.

Grant came over to stand by her side. "That's right. It wasn't exactly convenient."

"Scarcely on a honeymoon itinerary, eh?" Bart took a leather cigar case from his coat pocket. "Well, I hate to be the one to call you down from the clouds, but last quarter's balance sheet is pretty discouraging." He clipped off the end of his cigar and took up a silver lighter from the desk top. "I hope you can persuade your bride to be sensible and sell out her interest in this plant, Grant. There's no sense losing any more money and that Midwest offer is about to expire."

"Just a minute," the younger man said firmly. "I'm strictly an outsider in all this."

"Not any more, you're not," Winthrop told him. "You've dealt yourself into the game."

79

"Well—in that case, Jean's not folding until I've looked at the cards."

"Not even if I can get those Chicago people to raise the ante?" Bart's eyebrows drew down and he shifted his cigar to the corner of his mouth. "I hoped my experience would count for something. There isn't time for a 'do it yourself' course in plywood manufacturing, young man."

A surge of red showed on Grant's cheekbones at the implied criticism, but he remained silent.

"And how do you feel about this, Jean?" Bart asked with a probing glance from under his heavy lids.

"I thought you'd never ask." Her smile masked any undertones. "I'll go along with Grant. After all, he is my husband and that was the whole idea of my uncle's will—to let the man decide. You know that."

Bart pursed his lips and nodded reluctantly. "Well, we'll postpone any decisions for the time being, but there are some papers for you to sign, Grant." He nodded toward a pile of documents in the middle of his desk blotter. "You'll find they're in compliance with the formalities of your marriage. The responsibility for the estate shifts out of my hands now and into yours."

Grant took the pen he handed him. "Does this mean that I'm acceptable as a spouse? From your executor's standpoint, of course."

"I knew what you meant," Bart told him dryly. "You're quite acceptable but I must confess I'd rather have you working for me. Maybe we can arrange that too."

Grant finished putting his signature on the papers. "Maybe," he said noncommittally. "Right now, I'm more interested in getting on with my honeymoon. As long as we're here though, I'd like to take a quick tour of the plant."

"Of course," Bart said. "I'd go with you except there's a lot of work for me to get through. Right now I'm trying to get to the bottom of that fire we had the day before yesterday."

"I didn't think it caused any damage," Jean said.

"Not much in dollars but plenty in morale. Even the key employees are beginning to suspect trouble."

Jean tucked her purse under her arm. "I promise to look cheerful when we make the grand tour."

"It's no joking matter," Bart said, moving back to his desk chair. "Foster's had to replace two members of the bull gang in the last two weeks because they don't like the long-range job prospects here. It would be good if we could get together for dinner and discuss this. I'll be glad to hear Grant's ideas."

Jean looked up at the tall figure beside her. "Had you made any plans for tonight?"

His lips quirked. "I'm not going bowling with the boys if that's what you mean."

"Let's go to the Inn," Bart said, ignoring undertones. "You'll be my guests, of course."

"You'd better let us entertain you at the house," Jean told him. "That way Doreen can join us."

The other stirred uneasily. "It was nice of you to let her stay on. She wouldn't listen when I told her to confirm a room at the Inn before we left California. Takes after her mother's side of the family. Hard-headed."

Jean's glance was amused. "Not her uncle's side?"

He raised his thick eyebrows reprovingly. "Certainly not. By the way, Grant—I'd appreciate the use of the cottage for one more night and then I'll turn it back to you. My favorite room at the Inn won't be ready until tomorrow and under the circumstances, I didn't think I'd be inconveniencing you."

If Grant was discommoded, it didn't show in his expression. "Make yourself at home." He opened the door for Jean. "Let's get on with the tour. I have an appointment with an agate beach at low tide."

"Take him away," Bart said, waving them out. "Makes me wish I was young again myself. I'll see you about six-thirty if that's all right, Jean."

"Fine," she assured him. "If the weather holds, we'll have cocktails on the patio."

"See you later." Grant closed the door behind them as they went out into the hall. "Where do we go first?"

"I suppose we should start with the sawmill." Jean hesitated a minute as they reached the main door of the office wing. "We don't have to do this now if you'd rather get down to the beach."

He held the door and motioned her through. "That comment was merely for window dressing," he said enigmatically. "Lead on to the sawmill."

"This way, then. We'll go up that steep flight of stairs ahead of us. There's a raised catwalk so you can view the proceedings. We've put up explanatory signs at some of the vantage points because there's so much noise from the machinery."

"I expect a better tour than that," he said whimsically.

"Very well, Mr. Stevenson, you'll get the deluxe buildup." She cleared her throat dramatically as they started up the steps. "Before they get to this phase of the operation, the logs are brought down from the hills and stored in a sort yard to be graded . . . about a half mile away. After the grading, they're put in what's called a 'cold deck.' At this point, some of them are shipped directly to purchasers from the Asian countries. The remaining logs are debarked hydraulically and put in our millpond over there." She gestured down toward the water to their left. "When the logs are ready to be used, they're yanked into the mill and cut according to the best usage for that particular kind of timber. In the mill you'll see the head saw, the bull edger, the cut-off saw . . ."

"You're losing me. . . ." he warned.

She nodded understandingly. "Actually I can talk a pretty good game, but you'll have to ask Mr. Foster or Bart if you have any difficult questions." She paused at a swinging door by the head of the stairs. "From now on, it's practically sign language in this building because the saws make such a racket cutting through the logs."

"Right." Grant pushed open the door and motioned her through. He noted her shiver as the cold, damp air from the mill surrounded them and made a resolve not to linger. Obviously her thin outfit wasn't the ideal

82

costume for touring sawmills. Seeing the bulky clothing the employees were wearing, he was wishing for a padded nylon jacket himself as the cold drafts eddied around their catwalk.

The banshee wailing of the saws as they cut into the logs and the sour smell of wet wood made the atmosphere almost satanic. Watching timbers five feet in diameter being sliced down like a piece of bologna was both awe-inspiring and frightening. The shrieking saw blade seemed almost human and Grant found himself wincing instinctively as the first mammoth cuts were made. But it wasn't until they had passed out of the main wing of the mill and were in the comparative quiet of the saw-filing room that he spoke. "Now I really *do* feel as if I'm in the Crazy House at an amusement park." He gestured toward the lethal bands of steel stacked on the tables around them. "This place would make a vampire run screaming in the opposite direction. How big are these things?"

"This particular saw is eighteen inches wide and runs fifty-five feet in circumference." She touched one of the razor-sharp points with a cautious fingertip. "Properly cared for, they last about a year. The saw filers could tell you more about them." She looked around the room casually. "They're probably off on a break now."

"I'd need a break if I worked here." Grant was fascinated by a blade jerking past a nearby automatic sharpening device. "Those teeth look like a line of daggers. The whole thing could pass as an instrument of torture from the Spanish Inquisition."

Jean smiled understandingly. "It all depends on your point of view. The men here see it as a piece of the finest Swedish steel and keep a sharp watch for metal fatigue."

Grant grinned slowly in response. "I stand corrected." He surveyed the rest of the room with saws of all sizes hanging from wall pegs and coiled on long wooden benches. "But I still say it's the perfect site for a horror movie. Let's get out of here."

"I don't take much convincing on the subject," she assured him, leading the way to a door on the far side of the room. "If we go down these stairs, we can cut across the yard and you can see the plywood operation." She took a deep breath as they went out in the air. "Ummm—that smells good."

"The sun feels good too." Grant glanced at her anxiously. "Hadn't we better find a coat for you before we do any more touring? That outfit of yours wasn't meant for such things."

"What kind of an outfit *would* double for a wedding dress and touring a sawmill?" she asked flippantly, trying to disregard a sudden tight feeling in her throat.

Grant's lips compressed to the familiar grim line. "You're right, of course," he said finally, "but I wasn't being critical. The inside of that mill felt like a barn with all the doors left open."

"The doors will be open here too," she acknowledged, indicating a sprawling frame building in front of them. "The only amenities are for the logs—Bart will tell you that. They're treated very carefully."

"Does the mill operation make money?" He shortened his stride to make walking on the rough path easier for her.

"So I'm told. It's only the plywood part of the operation that Bart wants to dispose of. Otherwise he claims that it will take all the profit from the mill to keep solvent. He'll undoubtedly bring all the facts and figures to dinner tonight. I strongly suggest that you eat first before you let him ruin your appetite." She went on in a lower tone. "Probably I should have shown you the financial statement before we got married. At least I'll be a whale of a deduction on your income tax."

"I don't think most bridegrooms demand a credit rating," he replied coolly. "My mother instructed me never to discuss politics, money, or religion with a woman."

"What *do* you discuss with one?"

He glanced at his watch. "At three o'clock in the afternoon—practically nothing. Why are we stopping here?"

"To put on a hard hat." She indicated the white plas-

84

tic headgear stacked on a counter outside the building. "Not that you need one," she said sarcastically, still annoyed by his change of subject.

He reached over and dropped one on her hair before getting another for himself. "You're mistaking determination for . . ."

"Hardheadedness. You bet I am!" She waggled her headgear experimentally for size. "Why is it that you never take me seriously?"

"My mother also told me to avoid the words 'never' and 'always,' " he said whimsically as he widened the gap in the sliding door. "Watch the step!" he warned as she plunged past him. He caught her arm just in time to save her from landing on her nose. His lips were twitching as he watched her brush herself down. "Hurt yourself?"

"My pride is frayed and there's a big dent in my self-control, but thanks for saving my nylons."

"My pleasure." That elusive spark of humor flickered again as he watched her. "You were going to tell me about the financial drain that I've married into."

Jean stared hard at him for a minute. "I wish," she said finally, "that I knew what you were thinking." She put up a hand before he could reply. "Don't bother answering that. I don't think I'd believe you anyhow."

He gave her a long look. "Let's leave it under unfinished business for now. Later on, perhaps I can convince you." He glanced at his watch. "There's not much time. . . ."

"Never the time and the place," she quoted softly.

"Watch it—you're not the only one to read Browning," he cautioned. "Women pick the damndest times to go off on a tangent. I thought you were going to tell me why you and Bart Winthrop are losing a bundle on this plywood operation."

She made a futile gesture toward the sheets of plywood stacked high on either side of them. "If I knew why we were losing so much money," she said with some asperity, "I'd be happy to tell you. All I've heard is that foreign competitors have undercut our prices and taken most of the market."

He frowned. "That doesn't sound like the whole answer."

"Maybe you'll find a better one when we tour through. We'll start down by the lathe so you can see the beginning of the operation right after the logs are brought into the plant. Better move over," she cautioned, guiding him closer to the plywood stacks as a forklift operator zipped past. "These fellows aren't expecting to find anyone in their path and believe me, this is one place where the pedestrian does *not* have the right of way."

"Thanks for the warning." He watched another towering load pass them. "You saved me from being skewered."

She smiled sympathetically. "Actually he would have missed you—but it was close. It's better if we go single file and stay next to the stacks. When we get down by the heavy machinery, you can't even hear the forklifts coming." She led off carefully. "Most of the noise is from the big lathe," she said, raising her voice. "It can peel off thicknesses of wood ranging from one thirty-second to a quarter inch. Then it goes to the clipper operator and is sorted according to width."

"I can't say much for the odor," he complained as the sour stench of wet wood hit them. "It's as bad as the mill."

She nodded and motioned for him to watch the long ribbon of wood feeding off the lathe and being trimmed by the clipper operator into marketable pieces. Once sorted by width, the sections were forklifted and taken down to be fed into the mammoth drier.

Grant waited until they were snaking a new log on the lathe and comparative quiet reigned. "How long does it take these sections to go through the drier?" he asked.

"Anywhere from ten minutes to over an hour—depending on the thickness of cut and the type of wood. When they come out, there's less than five percent moisture remaining in the wood. We'll go down to the end."

He strolled beside her down past the area where sections were put on a conveyor belt leading into the huge oven. "It looks like a variation of a giant rotisserie!"

"I know what you mean." She shuddered graphically. "It would be terrible to fall onto that belt by mistake. You'd end up like a serving of shish kabob." She edged around a discard bin. "Let's move on down. Women sorters do the final grading when the wood comes out of the drier. They put it in bins that have names like 'Fishtail,' 'Core,' and 'Center.' I'll be darned if I can see any difference, but they seem to."

Grant grinned briefly. "Your talents lie in other directions."

"Mmmm—that's a diplomatic way of putting it." She stopped suddenly as they entered a dingy room. "I guess this plugging room's deserted. We should have asked Bart if the fire caused any real damage in this part. You can still smell the aftereffects, but everything's so grimy that it's hard to tell whether it got that way from old age or smoke smudge."

He approached two good-sized pieces of machinery standing in the center of the room. "What are these?"

"Pluggers." She saw his puzzled expression and went on to explain. "It's where they cut out knots in the plywood and fill with wooden plugs to upgrade the finished product. One machine makes round plugs and the other makes boat-shaped ones."

"No round plugs for square holes?" Grant wanted to know and ducked as she reached for a small piece of wood in the waste bin.

"You'd better hide after a remark like that," she said severely, "but I was just going to show you that we even utilize our waste. This is all sold to a pulp mill up north." She dropped the block back into the bin and dusted her hands. "We mix our own glues too, but that section is shut down this late in the afternoon. That's where they feed in a cross-grain core and it's glued on both sides. From then on, they merely add the specified number of panels or plys for the finished product. And that concludes my lecture for the afternoon," she said, bobbing down in a mock curtsy.

"Very nicely done too," he said solemnly.

"Thank you, sir. All compliments will be passed along to the management and any gratuities will be gratefully received."

They had retraced their route to emerge by the main entrance and she paused to slip off her hard hat and put it with the others.

"It's a pity you have to give that back." Grant deposited his headgear next to hers. "You might set a new style trend."

"I already have. For a going-away costume, the bride wore gold with white accessories. *Women's Wear Daily* please copy."

"I shouldn't have taken mine off," he told her, gripping her elbow to help her over a muddy patch on the path. "The way you talk makes me feel that a hard hat is a real necessity."

"It's easy to see that you're quivering with fear." She drew her elbow away carefully, disliking the confused feeling that close contact with Grant gave her. Deliberately she changed the subject. "Where in the dickens did the guard put your car?"

"There it is—half hidden by the building. If he'd put it any further away, we might as well have walked from town."

They proceeded in silence until they came up beside it.

He reached over to open the door. "Do you mind if we stop off in town? I'd like to talk to your friend Toby. It shouldn't take long if he's in his office."

"I don't mind," her voice was hesitant, "but I really should get home and make arrangements for dinner. Mrs. Lloyd doesn't even know how many there will be."

"That's easy to solve." He went around the front of the car and opened the other door. "You can drive and take the car on up to the house."

She paused before getting in. "But what about you? How will you get back from town?"

He slid into the passenger seat. "No problem there.

88

I can hitch a ride from Toby or call Doreen. She's bound to have made connection with some form of transportation by now."

She took the ignition key he handed her. "You needn't go to all that trouble. I could come back down and pick you up after I settle the menu." She was checking the rear-view mirror before reversing out onto the driveway.

"Hey, watch it! There's some character right behind you."

"I see him," she said, braking gently and allowing the man to enter a side door of the office building. "He should pay more attention to where he's going or he'll never make it to his next birthday." She craned her head to peer after the disappearing figure. "He's new around here. Must be one of the replacements for the bull gang."

"What does that term mean?"

"General laborers. Most employees start there and work up." She eased the car ahead and then turned to look at the silent figure beside her. "What's the matter? You look as if the weight of the world had suddenly dropped on your shoulders."

He shook his head impatiently. "It was that workman. I just caught a glimpse of him but I could swear that I've seen him before."

"Well, he's new to this neighborhood." She accelerated as she pulled out onto the main highway. "I hope that Toby's in a better mood than he was last night. Otherwise he might give you a bad time."

Grant refused to be drawn. "I don't anticipate any trouble. He's had plenty of time to get over being a disappointed suitor."

"That's not very flattering to me," she pointed out with some asperity, "or don't you believe in people carrying torches?"

"Not if there isn't any point to it."

She gave her attention to a school bus which cut in her lane and considered his terse reply. "Maybe Toby will feel differently," she said eventually to break the uneasy silence. "After all, we've been friends for quite a while."

"We'll see." He was patently disinterested. "Just let me out on the corner by his office, will you. There's no need for you to wait."

"I suppose I shouldn't ask what you plan to discuss with him either?"

He looked amused as she pulled abruptly over to the curb. "Strictly business. No duels will be fought today. Take it easy on the drive home until you get the feel of the brakes on this car. Seems to me you're hitting them too hard."

Feminine pride surged to the fore. "Now I'm getting driving lessons. . . ."

"I didn't say you needed them," he assured her blandly as he got out and closed the door. He bent down to the open window. "Just don't be lead-footed on the brakes. Let me know if you want me to pick up any groceries." He gave her a brief gesture of farewell and strode off.

Jean stared after him in stunned amazement. Talk about masculine taking-over! Grant Stevenson must have invented the term. If he had seemed assured before, the marriage ceremony had certainly strengthened that assurance.

Her lips thinned in annoyance as she pulled out into the traffic once again. She let the car move slowly along Main Street as she thought about the day's events. In all fairness she had to admit that Grant's backing had been welcome during the interview with Bart. Call it male arrogance or whatever, the older man didn't attempt to ride roughshod over his new partner.

She made a grimace of distaste as she glanced in the rear-view mirror. Life had become topsy-turvy ever since Grant's six-foot figure had loomed up out of the surf. Despite his pronouncement that he was a husband "in name only," he had taken over the leading reins with a vengeance. Moreover, he showed no signs of relinquishing them. To be strictly impartial . . . did she want him to?

Still engrossed in the puzzle, she pulled carefully around to pass a pint-sized cyclist. Then she honked and waved at Rick, who glanced up to give her a sur-prised grin in return as he recognized Grant's car.

As she drove on, she realized that Rick wouldn't be the only person surprised at seeing her drive up in the gleaming Thunderbird. Satisfying Mrs. Lloyd's curios-ity about her new status could take the rest of the after-noon. Perhaps it would have been better to go out to dinner, after all.

Jean slowed and signaled for a left turn down the steep dip to her private driveway. The brake pedal re-sponded poorly and she thought of Grant's last-minute instructions. "Lead-footed" indeed!

Anger made her swerve off onto the winding drive more abruptly than usual. Immediately after the turn-off, the gravel tracks plunged in a downward curve for fifty feet before climbing in switchbacks to the top of the hill. The Thunderbird fishtailed on the shallow ruts as it pointed down and Jean braked strongly to keep the heavy car on the drive.

It took only a horrified moment to realize that her foot had shoved the limp brake pedal all the way to the floor and that the car was picking up speed rather than slowing. Unless she could brake it in some way there wasn't a chance of staying on the road.

Desperately she weighed her only two choices: a steep cliff-face to the left plunging sharply to the beach or the more gentle wooded slope to the right. Her knuckles whitened as they clutched the steering wheel. There was no choice—not if she wanted to live. And the decision had to be now!

She pulled the wheel to the right—scarcely hearing the tangled underbrush scraping against the body of the car as the ravine bottom flashed into view. She yanked on the wheel again—anything to avoid the cliff-face at the left. Then suddenly there was the shriek of tearing metal as the car collided with the trunk of a towering fir tree.

Jean endured only a split second of pain when she was thrown against the windshield before consciousness fled. The long black car slithered sideways to a stop . . . crumpled and torn near the base of the tree.

There was a short period of time until the debris settled and then only the rumble of the surf below broke the stillness of the afternoon.

Chapter SIX

In the hours that followed, a confused jumble of heads flickered in and out of Jean's vision.

An anxious-looking Grant registered momentarily and then was exchanged for Toby's concerned visage. Doreen's fragile countenance appeared and then it was Bart's lined face hovering overhead. Finally there was another gray-haired man who looked vaguely familiar. He said something she couldn't understand and smiled encouragingly before a sharp prick in her arm let a merciful cloud settle back down.

When she awakened the next time, it was in the familiar surroundings of her yellow and white bedroom. Although the blinds were partially drawn, bands of sunlight edged the rug and climbed onto the foot of her bed.

"Good morning." Grant's long length unfolded from the chair by the window and he put aside the paper he had been reading. "The doctor said you should be coming around about now. Let me help you with those pillows so you can sit up properly." He came to the side of the bed and bending down, supported her shoulders while deftly tucking two pillows behind her back. "There . . . is that better?"

"Yes, thanks." Jean's mind felt as if it were still wrapped in layers of cotton and only partially functioning. Her eyes clouded as memories came slowly seeping back. "The car . . . I thought I couldn't stop it. It was awful. . . ."

"Don't!" The mattress creaked under his weight as he sat down beside her. "It's all over now. How are you feeling?"

"I'm not sure. Sort of like a disembodied spirit." She put a hand up to her forehead and winced as she encountered a discernible lump. "What in the dickens did I hit?"

"My windshield and you lost the battle," he said. "Don't worry—the bruises will fade and the doctor says you'll be back to normal in a few days."

"It's still pretty much of a blur. I can just remember snatches of what happened."

He nodded. "Rick heard the crash and went for help. That young man has a good head on his shoulders. The neighbors up on the road put in an emergency call for the doctor."

"How did you and Toby hear about it?"

"It was the damndest thing. Bart had an appointment with the same doctor and arrived at the office just as he came tearing out. When he heard the location of the accident, Bart forgot about his blood pressure and followed in his car. He saw Toby and me standing in front of the Development Corporation office and bundled us in."

"Thinking you might be interested."

His eyebrows climbed at her dry tone. "Something like that. At any rate, you'd assembled quite a crowd when we arrived practically on the doctor's rear bumper. Once he decided you could sleep off the effects of your bump on the head at home, things settled down a bit. I'm to drive you up to the hospital as soon as it's convenient so they can take precautionary X-rays."

Jean shuddered visibly. "I don't ever want to get in a car again."

"Try to forget the whole thing."

"Forget about it!" Her voice rose in a wail. "That's
94

easy for you to say. Why didn't you tell me your brakes were bad instead of criticizing my driving?" Her attention was suddenly distracted by the flowing sleeve of her nightgown as she gestured. "And how the dickens did I get into this nightgown?" she asked accusingly. Belatedly she slid under the sheet as she remembered the transparency of the bodice.

He sighed audibly. "Doreen and Mrs. Lloyd did the honors, so you don't have to blush."

"I'm not blushing. Look—would you please find a bedjacket for me in the closet. I feel like a mummy wrapped in this sheet."

He rose obediently, but said, "I don't know what you're making such a fuss about. We *are* married."

"We merely share the same marriage license—there is a difference," she replied dryly and then went back to her original question. "Why didn't you tell me the brakes were defective?"

"They weren't." His voice was muffled as he searched through hangers. "They were working perfectly in the morning."

"I don't understand. Are you crazy or am I?" She ran a hand distractedly through her tousled hair. "When I tried to slow down, the brake pedal went right to the floor. It was spongy before but I thought the brakes just needed adjusting."

"I gathered that's what happened." He gave the hangers a final impatient twitch and turned around. "The only thing that looks like a bedjacket in here is pink satin. It won't do much for that leopard print nightgown."

Her answering look spoke volumes. "Just hand me the black sweater from the top drawer of my bureau, please."

"I don't know why I bother," he grumbled. "Frankly, I like that nightgown the way it is. You must be feeling better or you wouldn't be so particular."

"And you must be feeling guilty or you wouldn't be changing the subject."

"Guilty—hell!"

"Don't shout. You'll have the house down on us."

She flounced irritably under the sheet. "What else am I to think? You get out of the car and whammo—there I am playing 'Thread the Needle' with the fir trees."

"Very funny." He unearthed the black cardigan and tossed it over to her. "In case you're wondering, the tree came out in better shape than you did."

"How's the car?"

"Being fixed. I had them check the brakes first thing."

Her hands stilled in the process of buttoning the cardigan. "And?" she asked.

"Someone had damaged the master brake cylinder in such a way that it would operate with light braking but on a steep hill it would rupture and the car would go out of control."

She sank back against the pillows, her cheeks as white as the snowy linen cases. "You mean it was deliberate?"

"That's right." He strode restlessly over and perched on a corner of the dressing table. "What I can't figure out is whether they were aiming for both of us . . ."

"Or just you or me." There was a moment of silence before she went on. "There was only one time when anyone could have tampered with that brake cylinder."

"At the plant." He nodded. "I figured that out too. In fact, I've gone over it piece by piece. First, the guard moved the car to an isolated spot. . . ."

"You can't accuse that guard. He's lived here for fifty years and worked at the plant for the last twenty. Why, the Sea Bend PTA even named him 'Grandfather of the Year.' "

"I wasn't accusing him," Grant said patiently, "but your reasoning escapes me. Benedict Arnold was probably a grandfather too."

"He didn't live in Sea Bend. . . ."

"I didn't say he did. I can't see what difference . . ." he raked a hand impatiently through his hair. "Oh, for God's sake, let's get off the subject."

She folded her arms across her breast but only succeeded in looking pale and defiant rather than achieving the casual air of sophistication she hoped for. "Why

96

is it that men get angry every time they get in a logical discussion with a woman?"

"I'll tell you sometime. Right now we've left the car being parked behind the building." He frowned in concentration. "It could have been a spur-of-the-minute thing, I suppose. Who knew we were going to be out at the plant?"

"Lots of people . . . it wasn't a secret," she pointed out. "Bart made the appointment at the Inn last night. Toby heard him, Doreen, maybe even Ernie. Then there were the workmen at the mill. One of them could have done the job while we were in the plywood section."

His frown deepened. "There was that fellow we saw when we were leaving."

"The one I didn't recognize?" She looked thoughtful. "Why don't you ask Bart about him?"

"Maybe I will. I could swear he looked familiar."

"Well, if Bart can't help, the personnel department at the mill could give you his past record. Although if he goes around wrecking cars, I doubt if he advertises his talent."

Grant made a snort of derision.

She plucked at the turned-down sheet. "I wonder if they'll try again?" Her tone was deliberately offhand.

"It would be nice to know." There was a pause and then Grant looked up with an apologetic grimace. "Hell! I'm sorry. I shouldn't be worrying you with this now."

"Don't be silly. I'm going to get dressed and rejoin the human race."

"Not until the doctor calls you aren't. He said he'd look in after his hospital rounds."

"What time is it now?"

He glanced at his watch. "Quarter to eleven. You've been flat out since yesterday afternoon."

"How did you all manage last night?"

"Doreen and Mrs. Lloyd did all the work. Toby, Bart, and I stuck around getting in the way."

She nodded and then got out the question which really interested her. "Where did you sleep?"

If Grant was amused by her directness, he didn't let on. "There's no need for you to be concerned. I was on the davenport for part of the night and in the chair here for the rest of it. Doreen and I took turns keeping an eye on you."

"That was kind of you," she mumbled, wishing she could feel more enthusiastic about life in general.

In front of her, the sun streamed cheerfully onto the rug, out in the hall the delightful aroma of coffee was making itself known, by her side one of the handsomest men she'd ever seen was evidently prepared to indulge her every whim, and she sat in the middle of all the luxury feeling like a grubby displaced person.

Getting mixed up with Grant was like falling in the river while fleeing from a rainstorm. Emotionally it was an absolute catastrophe. And noting Grant's complacent look at the moment, he not only had escaped the drenching—he hadn't even gotten his feet wet.

She sighed gustily.

"What's the matter?" He paused by the door to look back at her. "Feeling miserable?"

She nodded, wishing they accepted women recruits in the Antarctic.

"I suppose you have a fiendish headache?"

She nodded again, wondering what he'd say if she confessed it was heart trouble bothering her at the moment. Probably he'd take the first plane to California.

"Never mind—you'll feel better after some breakfast," he said calmly. "I'll tell Doreen to start boiling an egg for you. Your headache won't stand a chance." He closed the door behind him.

She leaned back against the pillows and smiled grimly. A cup of coffee and an aspirin would undoubtedly do wonders for the headache, but she was at a loss to know what medication she could take for the other malady.

By the time breakfast arrived, Jean had slipped from the bed to wash her face and change into a pair of white nylon pajamas with a matching brunch coat. After a quick look at her bruised face in the mirror, she decided white was the best color to choose. Otherwise she'd have needed a Jacob's coat to blend with her many hues.

Doreen was still exhibiting company manners and couldn't have been nicer. Jean looked at the dainty breakfast tray and made a mental resolve to reform as well.

"I'm glad you're feeling better," Doreen told her frankly as she put the tray carefully across her knees. "You have no idea what a flap you caused last night. Do you mind if I have coffee with you?" She took an extra mug from the tray and cradled it in her hands. "Toby's at work and Grant went down to the cottage to feed his darned goldfish. What is it about that fish anyhow? I've never known Grant to be so scrupulous about a thing like that before."

"He must be afraid of incurring Rick's wrath. He probably checks on Homer every time he delivers the paper."

Doreen went over to sit in the chair. "He's a nice youngster, isn't he? Thank goodness he kept his head yesterday. He was really the one responsible for getting help so quickly."

"That's what Grant said." Jean put her empty juice glass back on the tray and extracted a piece of toast from a covering napkin. "I must do something special to thank him."

"Decide on it quickly then. The young man's coming to check your state of health this afternoon." Doreen wriggled restlessly in her chair. "What am I sitting on?" She pulled out a pamphlet from the back of the cushion. "A Short History of Plywood," she read aloud and then tossed it on the lamp table. "Doesn't sound like the ideal bedtime companion to me."

"Grant was reading it, I guess."

"Oh!" There was sudden understanding in Doreen's tone. "He must have gotten it from Toby. They were huddled in some business discussion for hours after Bart went back to the cottage." She got up to look in the dressing table mirror. "I was wearing a new green chiffon and it didn't get the slightest response from either of them." She inspected her flawless complexion carefully. "Do you suppose I'm starting to go to seed?"

Jean giggled at the absurdity of the statement. "If you are, I hope I can go just like you." She picked up a spoon and tried a bite of soft-boiled egg. "Toby can be difficult at times," she said tactfully.

"That's a diplomatic way of phrasing it. Do you know that we played nine holes of golf yesterday and he spent the entire time telling me what was wrong with my short game." She made a face in the mirror. "Even Uncle Bart manages to say something nice once in a while."

"Sounds as if Toby's down on women."

"Because of you and Grant, you mean?" Doreen nodded sagely. "He certainly didn't like having his romantic plans upset."

"Ummm—maybe." Jean finished the last bite of egg and touched at her lips with a napkin. "Actually I don't think Toby's emotions are involved. I've felt all along that I was just part of an attractive real estate parcel to him. If he could get some of this hill for building lots, he'd probably be happier the way things are."

"What he needs is to fall in love," Doreen agreed. "*Really* in love, I mean."

"Why don't you give it a whirl?" Jean challenged.

"I don't know why I bother." Doreen went back to collect her coffee mug. "There are scads of men at home."

Jean smiled gently. "A little resistance adds zest to the chase and he *is* awfully nice."

"Oh, I'll give it a try. After all, you brought Grant to heel and he was a really difficult case." She reached over to pick up the breakfast tray. "I'd better collect Mrs. Lloyd's shopping list if we're going to eat tonight."

"That's wonderful of you. My car keys are on the hall table."

"There's no problem about transportation," Doreen assured her. "Grant has a rental car until his is fixed and Toby said he'd come by later on."

"In that case, I'd say you were doing very well. I've never known Toby to offer his services at the supermarket before."

"There has to be a first time for him to learn to be human. Oops, there's the doorbell." She paused halfway out to the hall. "Are you receiving callers?"

"Of course. Your breakfast has made a new woman of me."

"Not that!" Doreen gave her a cheeky grin. "Grant would have my head. I'll see you later—if the doctor orders any invalid's menus just send them down to the kitchen."

After the doctor had completed a thorough examination, he fortunately did not order any invalid's menus. He merely said, "Keep on with the bed rest for this afternoon. Your husband will bring you in for X-rays tomorrow morning." He patted her shoulder gently. "You'll feel much better when those abrasions and bruises heal."

"In the meantime, take two aspirin, keep warm, and call your office if anything develops."

His frown turned to an amused look as he interpreted her demure expression. "Exactly, young lady. Any more questions?"

"Not a one. Thank you for coming so quickly yesterday, Doctor."

He cleared his throat. "Can't have our hospital librarians out of service, you know. We need you. I'll leave instructions for the X-rays tomorrow." His grizzled face cracked in a youthful grin as he picked up his bag. "Be sure and phone if you run out of aspirin. I have some samples I'll be glad to sell you."

"Remind me to report you to the A.M.A."

He merely waved cheerfully and disappeared down the hall.

Evidently he met the next caller on the front porch because when Rick was shown into the bedroom he said solemnly, "The doctor told me you were feeling better and he thought you were receiving visitors— but that I should ask to be sure."

"I'm sure," Jean told him. "I've been hoping you'd

come so that I could thank you for all your help yesterday."

"Gee, that's okay, Miss Cam . . . I mean, Mrs. Stevenson." He grinned suddenly and shed his dignity in the process. "My mom says that's what I have to call you from now on." He stuck his hands in his jean pockets and strolled over to the wide window to peer out. "Boy—you can see a long way from here. Is Mr. Stevenson going to come and live in this house or will you go down to his cottage?"

"I really don't know," Jean admitted, wishing she did. Trust Rick to get right down to the heart of things. She sat up straighter and decided to change the subject for her own protection. "How about some cookies and milk?"

"No thanks. Mrs. Lloyd said she'd have some in the kitchen for me when I left." Doggedly he went back to his original subject. "I s'pose you'd have plenty of room in this big house for all of Mr. Stevenson's stuff? That's if he decides to come up here." His anxious expression contrasted with his casual tone.

"I suppose so." Jean felt her way carefully. "Just what did you have in mind?"

"Homer," Rick said succinctly. "He and Mr. Stevenson have sort of gotten used to each other by now."

"There's no doubt about that. Mr. Stevenson makes a special trip down to the cottage each day to see how he's doing."

"I know. Then you wouldn't mind if he brought him up here?"

"Homer could take his choice of tables in the living room. We might even change that pickle jar for an aquarium if it's all right with you."

"Swell!" The towhead let out a gusty sigh of relief.

"It's all settled then." She wriggled her toes under the comforter. "Now, let's get down to business, Rick. I'd like to get you a present. Is there anything special you want? Maybe something for Max. . . ."

"But that's all taken care of," he burst out. "Mr. Stevenson's having a glass cage built—he was going to put in the order today. It'll have a special feeding section and everything 'cause iguanas make such a mess when they eat."

"Really?"

He nodded in adult fashion. "Max sleeps right on the lettuce leaves, but this cage is going to have room for a driftwood log so he can climb up on it." His freckled face took on a rapt look. "Mr. Stevenson went to my school and talked to the principal and my science teacher. They're going to make Max a permanent exhibit for the Science Department. The principal's going to meet with the PTA ladies and see if they'll hold a benefit dinner every year to raise money for Max's food bill." He bounced down on the side of her bed. "How about that?"

"Couldn't be better." Jean smiled and reached up to tousle his hair. "If you need any other donations, just let me know."

"That's what Mr. Stevenson said too." Suddenly shy, he traced a pattern on the edge of the comforter. "It's sure swell of you both."

"Well, it was sure swell of you to take charge yesterday," she told him seriously.

He brushed the compliment aside. "Oh, everybody helped then—even if they were pretty excited. Ernie says that's the reason Mr. Winthrop was shouting at Mr. Stevenson."

She leaned forward. "Was this after the accident?"

"Yeah. It was after they'd brought you up here and while they were waitin' for the wrecker to come and get Mr. Stevenson's car."

She bit down hard on her lower lip to steady it. "And they were quarreling?"

He nodded emphatically. "You bet! Ernie was telling my folks later that you could hear Mr. Winthrop three blocks away shouting that he was going to file charges against Mr. Stevenson for gross negli . . . negl . . ." He struggled with the long word.

"Negligence?"

"That's right. And Mr. Stevenson told him to go right ahead but he wasn't in any position to be throwing stones." Rick was obviously enjoying his narrator's role.

103

"Mr. Winthrop shouted something about blackmail and he'd be damned if he'd pay any more money. . . ."

Jean felt her throat tighten at the ominous words and wished she had the courage to turn off his recital. Instead she asked, "Then what happened?"

He shrugged. "Mr. Stevenson saw me hanging around and said I'd better get on with my paper route."

"I see."

"You sure look pale all of a sudden. You feelin' sick?" he asked suspiciously.

"A little," she admitted.

"I'd better go," he said promptly. Then he remembered his manners and hesitated halfway out the door. "I'll tell Mrs. Lloyd you need help."

"No . . . don't bother," she protested but he was down the hall before she could get the words out. Her mind was still suffering a delayed reaction from Rick's story. Why had Bart accused Grant of blackmail, for heaven's sake? She reached over to turn her pillow and rested her forehead against the cool case. Blackmail! Did he mean it literally or was it just a figure of speech? And how could she explain to Mrs. Lloyd that her upset had nothing to do with the accident. Again she bit down hard on her lower lip to keep it from trembling. Tears wouldn't solve a thing and would merely further complicate any explanations.

Bart found her perched disconsolately on the side of the bed when he came into the room a few minutes later. "What was that boy saying about your being sick?" he wanted to know. "I thought the doctor reported you were better."

She swung her feet back under the covers and huddled against the pillows. "I'm not sick," she told him wearily. "Rick misunderstood me."

He grunted and went over to lower his ponderous bulk in the chair.

"You look very spruce," she told him, eyeing his gray and white jacket worn over a white linen vest.

He gave her a piercing look. "That's more than I can say for you. Your doctor was a little optimistic.

I told him yesterday that you should be taken to a hospital."

"Well, I'm glad he didn't listen to you," she said defiantly. "I couldn't get better treatment anywhere. Everybody's been wonderful."

"That may be," he admitted grudgingly, "but I feel it's still my responsibility. Especially now."

"Grant might have something to say about that."

"Good lord, girl—why do you suppose I'm pussy-footing about the way I am?" he blurted out. "He's had plenty to say already. That's why I'm concerned about your state of health."

"I don't understand. . . ."

His lips clamped into a thin line of displeasure. "Really Jean—such naïveté astounds me. I suppose that's why I wasn't more surprised when I heard about this hurry-up marriage of yours. It's just the kind of set-up that would appeal to an immature person like you."

She drew herself up stiffly. "Marriage to a responsible individual like Grant can hardly be termed as a whim . . . even by you."

"Well, it obviously isn't a whim as far as he's concerned," he said acidly. "That's why for your continued state of health I'm suggesting that you make a new will immediately."

"What the dickens are you talking about?"

He pointed an accusing finger at her. "In case it hasn't occurred to you—Oregon is a community property state rather than a dower rights one. As soon as you signed that marriage license, Grant could automatically collect one half of your assets. Since you have no close relatives, his share would be considerably more than half the estate. For someone who was already under a cloud of suspicion—marriage to you was like manna from heaven."

She kneaded her temples wearily. "I must be more dense than usual today. *What* cloud of suspicion?"

"I didn't think he'd told you about that," he shot out triumphantly.

"If you'd stop making accusations. . . ."

"All right," he interrupted, "I'll be glad to explain

105

it without any fancy wrappings. Your husband is on an enforced vacation up here because of some trouble in the company where he's employed." He folded his hands over his white vest and stared at her like an omniscient buddha. "Some weeks ago, there was an explosion in their laboratory and one of the employees was badly injured. As head of the department, Grant was naturally held responsible in case of negligence. Then the District Attorney questioned him because the police ruled it was a case of deliberate sabotage instead. Needless to say, Grant's employers aren't happy —their loss has run into thousands of dollars." He threw out his hands in an apologetic gesture as he noted her tense, unhappy expression. "You can't blame me for being suspicious of him under the circumstances. Why would a man with his background want a hasty marriage—even with a wealthy woman?"

"You're hardly flattering. . . ."

"I didn't mean to be," he said bluntly.

"Yet you apparently thought enough of his character and ability to offer him a job."

"Business is business. I have no trouble handling my employees and he is an excellent chemical engineer."

"Despite his expensive and careless mistakes."

"That explosion wasn't a mistake," he said baldly. "Now do you see · why I want you to make a new will?"

"Oh yes," her tone was equally dry, "you've been very graphic." She leaned back into the pile of pillows. "I'm still feeling rocky, Bart. You'll have to excuse me."

"Of course, my dear." He heaved his bulk out of the chair and came over to the bedside. "I'm sorry to give you such depressing news. Actually, I think Grant should have told you the facts of the case, but don't be too hasty in condemning him. He may have a perfectly valid excuse."

"I still wish he'd told me," she confessed miserably.

"I agree with you there. You can see now why I was concerned with your 'accident.' Be careful, Jean, that's all I ask." He went on earnestly. "Remember you can count on me."

"Thank you, Bart."

"I'll check with you later. With Doreen staying in the house, I have an excuse for keeping a close eye on both of you." He patted her shoulder awkwardly. "I'd get some sleep now if I were you."

Jean tried. For the next half hour she thrashed restlessly on the mattress but kept her eyes resolutely closed. If she could have closed off her whirling thoughts as well, sleep might have come. As it was, she only succeeded in feeling more miserable as time went on.

She was still tossing and turning when a knock came on the door and Doreen called softly from the hall.

"Are you awake in there? Grant's on the phone and wants to talk to you."

Jean started to reply and then closed her lips resolutely. Doreen whispered again, "Can you hear me?" before her footsteps finally faded back down the hall.

Only then did the huddled figure on the bed give up the struggle and turn to weep silently into her pillow.

Chapter *SEVEN*

"If I knew you better, I'd say you were acting like a stubborn mule," Doreen said pithily, "only I'm not sure whether there are lady mules. The sex life of donkeys and burros has always confused me."

"You're perfectly safe—I don't know anything about it either," Jean assured her.

"All right then, why don't you stop emulating one of the long-eared creatures and come to the Inn for dinner tonight. Grant told Toby to make reservations for the four of us."

"If Grant wants to go, he certainly can." Jean moved over to the living room window and stared out, avoiding the other's questioning glance. "You'll have to count me out, though."

"But why? The doctor thought you'd shrug off the effects of the accident easily. You've been moping around the house for the past five days."

"I'm sorry if I've inconvenienced you. . . ." Jean began stiffly and was interrupted by Doreen's plaintive wail.

" . . . That's what I mean. You act like a prickly pear most of the time. When you aren't locked in your bedroom, you're taking solitary walks on the beach—I don't think Grant's caught a glimpse of you in days. It's no wonder he moved back to the cottage. Even that darned goldfish would look good after the chilly atmosphere here." She strolled over and put a comforting arm around Jean's tense shoulders. "Come on, honey—what's the matter?"

Jean managed to laugh. "Heavens! All this because I don't want to go out to dinner. Don't make a federal case out of it, Dorrie. There's nothing the matter with me."

"All right." Doreen looked unconvinced but she passed it off. "It's just as well. Now I can send you down to pick up your husband's laundry. He forgot to bring it up this morning and Mrs. Lloyd won't want to be thrown off schedule."

"Damn! Why can't he. . . ?"

Doreen waggled an admonishing finger. "Remember what a jewel Mrs. Lloyd is before you make any drastic decisions. She expects the laundry collected today."

Jean sighed in defeat. "I know. All right, I'll go."

"That's good. Actually I'd do it for you except that I have a hair appointment down in the village."

"Go ahead. The walk will do me good."

"You don't have to walk. Grant rode with Toby this morning, so his car is outside."

"Where did they go today?"

"Beats me. If I ask Toby anything about his business, I find that I'm still listening two hours later." Doreen rooted in the hall closet and emerged clutching her car coat. "That's why I avoid early morning discussions."

Jean was amused. "When do you talk then?"

"Whenever my feminine instinct takes over. Generally it's when men are looking at you and you know they really see you—rather than just your new hairdo or the sheer blouse you're wearing." She grinned wickedly. "Not that both of those things don't help with Toby. I'm on a two-weeks' course to humanize him. The other night he went fifteen minutes without mentioning his corporation or a golf course. Grant thinks I'm doing very well."

"Why should his opinion matter?"

Doreen frowned and gave Jean a searching look. "You really *are* annoyed at him, aren't you?"

"Sorry." Jean was slightly shamefaced. "Are my prickles showing again? You'll have to forgive me."

"Pooh! Don't pay any attention to what I say." Doreen belted her coat and turned the collar up. "Toby says he tunes me out like a television commercial. I'd better get going. How about flank steak for your dinner tonight?"

"Fine," Jean said absently. "Before you go—where are Grant's car keys?"

"He said he'd leave the extra set in the glove compartment." Doreen caught up her purse from the hall table and checked her lipstick in the mirror above it. "Sure you can manage?"

"Of course. Have fun."

Doreen blew her a kiss and disappeared out the front door.

Jean indulged herself with an unnecessary cup of tea—knowing full well that she was deliberately postponing her visit to the cabin. Even without Grant's actual physical presence, it was painful raking over the memory of her night there. Who could have known that such a brief stay could plunge them into the maze of lies and evasions. If Bart's insinuations were true—or even founded on a particle of truth—then Grant had been a willing participant to the alliance. Even so, she reasoned, he could have told her the true story of his background. And if he had, an inner voice argued in return, would she have gone through with that hasty marriage?

Abruptly she got up from the breakfast table and took her cup and saucer over to rinse them in the sink. The best way to stop thinking was to go down and get the visit over with. In another week or so, she could safely broach the subject of an annulment to Grant. If he objected to the idea, she would retain a lawyer to work it out. And as for making a new will—

the way she was feeling at the moment, Grant was in far greater danger than she was. The man didn't have to make his dislike of her presence so blatantly obvious. No wonder her disposition had curdled.

She was still seething when she drove up by the cabin's back porch. Men! All they did was come around at strategic times to irritate women! She stomped up the porch steps. If the door was locked . . . and it probably was . . . Grant could worry about his own clean shirts. A momentary vision of him struggling with a hot iron and a wrinkled pile of laundry gleamed entrancingly. It was a distinct anticlimax to find the door opening easily to her touch.

She paused on the threshold and then walked slowly toward the front of the house, a slight figure in her beige-checked slacks with an Arran sweater flung carelessly over a white crew-necked shirt.

The living room was as welcoming as she remembered. She frowned as she ran her finger over the top of a table. It wasn't fair that he kept such a spic and span house. Men were supposed to wallow in untidiness when left to themselves. The remembrance of her own unmade bed back at the house deepened the frown. She was on the way to the kitchen when the sight of Homer's pickle jar drew her over to his corner of the room. The goldfish was moving in lethargic circles near the surface of the water.

"You look as if you're in the same mood as I am," she commiserated. "Life is hell, isn't it?" She watched him flip his tail and submerge to nibble a piece of green on the bottom. "I think, my friend," she told him appraisingly, "that you need some new vitamins in your fish food." Homer spit out the greenery and edged closer to the side of the jar. She knelt down to look him eye to eye. "How would you like a spanking new aquarium with fresh greens every week and a pretty lady goldfish to keep you company?"

"Stop turning his head," Grant said, pushing aside the sliding glass window next to the deck and sidling through. "What are you trying to do—win custody?"

111

Jean shot to her feet, her cheeks flaming. "You're not supposed to be here."

"Why not?" He calmly closed the glass to keep out the brisk salt breeze. "Remember your Shelley. . . ."

"What do you mean?"

"When a man marries, dies, or turns Hindu, his best friends hear no more of him," he quoted. "I only fit in one of the categories."

"Now you're being absurd." She turned away and started for the back of the house. "Doreen asked me to collect your laundry, but obviously there's been a mix-up somewhere."

He moved quickly to block her path.

She pulled back and gave him a scathing look. "Surely we're not going to play games."

A dull red crept along his cheekbones but he didn't move out of her way. "I'd rather we didn't," he said quietly. "It was bad enough persuading Doreen to get you down here."

"Why did you bother?"

"Because I wanted to find out why you've been avoiding me."

"Don't pretend you don't know." She shoved her hands deep in her slack pockets to hide their visible trembling. "Bart would be glad to set you straight— the way he did for me. He's a veritable fund of information. . . ."

"But not very good on public relations, I'll bet," he said deliberately.

"That's right. It would have been nice . . ." her voice faltered despite her effort to discipline it. "It would have been nice," she repeated, "to have heard the truth from you."

"Jean, listen," his hands moved up to clasp her shoulders. "At one time it wasn't important and later on when it was—there wasn't a proper time. I'd like to tell you my side of it now—if you'll please listen."

"When you put it like that," she assured him tremulously, "I can hardly refuse. All right—it would be fine to hear your side. For the past five days, I've been going around thinking you didn't have one."

Suddenly her head tipped forward to rest against his chest. "It's been awful."

"Poor Jean." His hand was gentle on her hair. "Why in the devil didn't you say something?"

"What? You don't go up to someone and ask if they married you for bail money."

An eyebrow arched. "Is that what I'm supposed to have done?"

"Among other things . . . and it isn't funny," she said severely, noting his amused expression.

"You're right about that. Come on. . . ." He took her elbows and steered her toward the kitchen. "We're going on a picnic and you'll have to carry part of the stuff. It's too nice a day to waste by staying indoors."

Puzzled, she glanced up at him. "Do you have anything to eat?"

He indicated a wicker hamper on the counter. "If you'll settle for tuna fish sandwiches, potato salad, and a slab of cheesecake."

"When did you get it all ready?" she asked, taking the blanket and cushions he was pushing at her.

"Mrs. Lloyd fixed it last night. You were the victim of a dark plot, my girl."

"I see. Was all this subterfuge necessary?"

He picked up the hamper and led the way to the door. "Since I hadn't seen anything but the back of your head for the better part of a week—I thought so. Watch the step," he cautioned as she moved off the porch. "Want me to carry the blanket?"

"Heavens no. I'm fine." She took a deep breath and for the first time became conscious of a beautiful spring day. Overhead, clouds scudded northward with the insistent Chinook wind setting the pace. The bent coastal junipers on the hillside waved their branches lazily in the stronger gusts as if marking time for the music of a rusty song sparrow nearby.

Grant checked his stride. "Can you make it to the top of the knoll?" he asked Jean. "It shouldn't take too long and the view is great."

"It sounds wonderful!"

"Good. Follow me . . . we'll cut through the pasture

113

here and go up the livestock path. The sheep must have held on by their teeth when they grazed on the top of this slope," he added after a few minutes' climb.

She tried to keep up with him and then fell back laughing. "You must be part mountain goat. Slow down or I'll miss the first course."

"Sorry." He shortened his stride and reached over to shore her up with a firm hand at her elbow. "I forgot that you were still a frail female."

"Any more remarks like that and I'll push you off the precipice. After I've saved the lunch, of course."

"Of course." He looked down into blue eyes shining with excitement. "I'd better not make any threats— even in jest—until I can convince you that I didn't have any ulterior motives in all this. Want to rest for a while?"

"No." She shook her head even though she was breathing hard. "It isn't far now and I'm ravenous."

"It's a good thing I commandeered plenty of sandwiches. Give me your hand here." He turned off the path and pulled her up a steep grassy slope. "What about spreading the blanket on that flat spot?"

"You must be a mind reader." She straightened as they reached the top and moved cautiously on the slippery grass to the spot he indicated. Then with her back to the breeze, she spread the blanket and anchored the two windward corners with pillows. "There," she said, collapsing gracefully on the third corner. "Bring on the food."

He obediently deposited the hamper between them but said, "No—sit back and relax" when she leaned forward to help unpack it. He undid plastic wrappings and carefully heaped two paper plates. "One for you and three for me," he counted aloud as he distributed the sandwiches.

"You wouldn't dare. . . ."

"Doctor's advice," he lied glibly, putting on three ripe olives as a finishing touch. "Overeating is bad for you."

"So is starvation."

He handed her a plate. "If you insist, madam—

there are extras for both of us. Mrs. Lloyd is a treasure of a cook."

"It's a pity she's married."

"Not really." He adjusted a pillow and rested his elbow on it. "So am I." He let the comment penetrate before picking up a sandwich and announcing, "No more conversation until lunch is over."

"Royal decree?"

"Precisely." The dignity of his proclamation was distinctly marred by a hefty bite of sandwich.

Jean hungrily followed suit.

They were on their second cup of coffee before Grant rescinded his ultimatum. He had lit a cigarette and watched Jean pursue a last crumb of cheesecake when he asked abruptly, "How much did Bart tell you about my job?"

Her eyes remained resolutely on the plate in her lap. "Not much, really. Just that you were in trouble with the District Attorney. . . ."

"I was *not* in trouble with the District Attorney," he interrupted acidly. "Naturally the law authorities wanted statements from the lab employees after the explosion at the plant. As the person in charge of that section, I made a statement too. The net result of all their investigation was that an explosive charge was planted by a person or persons unknown. Until our new quarters are ready in a couple of weeks, all of the laboratory staff is on leave. Doreen knew about the fracas in the plant and, of course, Bart did too. It was about that time that he made his job offer." Grant interrupted his recital to give her a whimsical look. "I can assure you that there are no warrants out for my arrest and that the District Attorney and I parted on very cordial terms."

She flushed. "I'm sorry to have doubted you. Obviously Bart was just telling part of the story."

"This isn't the first time, I'm afraid. He's been doing that in connection with the plywood plant too." Grant ground out his cigarette in the grass and disposed of the remains. "Toby and I have been trying to check the company books without calling for an

115

official audit. There's no reason the plywood division shouldn't be doing very well these days."

"Why do you say that?"

"Because of the impact of container shipping," he explained. "Plywood has really come into its own. With this prime northwest location, the company should be going great guns."

"What has location to do with it?"

"You should be supplying the trans-Pacific shipping companies and all the Alaskan freight people. Don't tell me that Bart's Midwestern business associates weren't thinking of that when they tendered their offer to buy."

"I wonder if there was any connection between that and the job offer Bart made to you?"

"Possibly." Grant shifted on the pillow and stretched out more comfortably. "The company I work for is his biggest competitor and our research is along the same lines. He knew that I'd been involved with special adhesives and they're important in the plywood business. With the container shipping, they've had to develop new resins for the reinforcing. They need substances that will prove resistant to corrosion and completely free from stress cracking. There's even a process in the wind to open up the plywood market still further in the future."

"Then why on earth has Bart been downgrading the plant?"

"Probably because he wanted to buy out your interest and Toby's interest as inexpensively as possible," he said succinctly. "At least, that's my guess. Remember, I can't prove any of this yet, but I can tell you that there is a tremendous future for the industry." Absently he reached out to grab a paper napkin which was caught in the breeze and carefully anchored it under the hamper. "Doreen had told Bart that I was up in this part of the country, but he had no reason to suspect that you and I even knew each other. When he met us at the Inn and heard our announcement, he looked like death itself. The last person he wanted you to marry was a research chemist."

116

"So he did his best to blacken your name. No, that isn't quite right," she admitted. "He just smudged it a little and left the rest to my imagination."

"If you'd like proof for my story, I'll give you the name of my chief at the plant and the member of the District Attorney's staff who did the questioning."

"Please don't . . ." she leaned over to put a hand on his arm. "You're making me feel like a dreadful heel."

"There's no need to," he said soberly, moving his hand up to grasp hers reassuringly. "After the experience you had, I'd be jittery too."

She frowned. "I can't see Bart involved in the brake business."

"I agree. He's not the type to roll around in the mud under a car. Besides, he has an alibi. Toby's secretary called the plant manager's secretary and found that Bart was in his office dictating most of the afternoon. Apparently he left the plant after we did to keep his doctor's appointment in town." He noted her raised eyebrows and explained. "High blood pressure. He has to keep getting it checked. Doreen told me the other night."

His strong tanned fingers clasping hers made every nerve end in her arm quiver, Jean decided. Not only that, the closeness of that rangy form was playing havoc with her breathing.

Under the pretense of searching for a handkerchief, she pulled herself up to a sitting position and moved a discreet distance away. She spoke lightly, avoiding his glance. "If Toby weren't showing such a decided interest in Doreen, I'd accuse him of it."

"Disappointed suitor tampers with car." His lips quirked in amusement as he shook his head. "Not this time. Right now Toby's incensed at the poor return on his plant investment. If we can show the profit picture has been tampered with—he'd be far more apt to throw Bart off the cliff."

"Not at Sea Bend. We keep our beaches tidy here." She dodged his lazy cuff at her. "All right—you've just eliminated two prime suspects. Who else is there?

117

Are you sure that you haven't figured in an unrequited love affair? After all, somebody blew up your lab and it was your car that was involved in the accident."

"I haven't had an unrequited love affair since I was twelve years old."

She tilted her head to one side like a curious bird. "That answer could be interpreted in different ways. Maybe I should have asked about the requited ones—or is there such a word?"

He gave her that lazy smile which always added to her confusion. "If you think I'm going to answer that . . . you're crazy. Want any more to eat or shall we pack up and go home?"

"No more. I'm stuffed now."

"I told you to skip that last half-sandwich."

"You begrudge me a measly half when you consumed at least four. . . ." She put the plastic cup back on the Thermos and waited for him to store it in the hamper.

"I was merely thinking of your waistline."

"Let me worry about that," she told him austerely.

"All right . . . but a waistline's pretty discreet. If you'd rather, I'll concentrate on another part like your . . ."

"Let's start down, shall we?" she cut into his sentence hastily and stood up, her cheeks glowing.

He reached out and held her close by his side. "When are you going to stop running? . . . There'll come a time when you can't escape so easily. You'll be missing a cot for the bedroom or a black sweater to hide behind." His eyes glinted. "Even a hill to run down."

She wrenched away, battening down her desire to stay close in that steely grasp. "When that day comes, I'll let you know."

"Do that," he agreed calmly. "Then I'll decide how I feel about it."

She looked up at him, startled, trying to gauge his enigmatic expression. Damn the man! Each time he

118

glanced at her in that way she felt as if she were going to explode in pieces.

"Shall we go," she mumbled finally, wishing she could think of an answer which would effectively put him in his place.

"By all means." He shouldered the blanket and piled the pillows in her arms. "Back to safety and civilization." Taking a last look at the magnificent coastline and the rugged crag of Wailing Rock, he added, "Or maybe civilization is up here. What do you think?"

Jean took a deep breath of the salt breeze and let her eyes follow the plump sea gulls swooping down to land on the rocky outcropping. In the pasture below them, a meadowlark whistled his cheerful measure and it sliced through the quiet air like a sharp blade. She became aware suddenly of the marvelous sense of solitude and, moving slowly, she leaned over to pull a seed stalk from a clump of tall grass and nibbled on the sweet end of it. This day, she dreamed, this hour, this place—I'll remember them always.

It was as if she'd spoken aloud.

"The time, the place . . ." Grant murmured at her side. "Remember?"

This time, the glance they exchanged was long and searching. Finally he grimaced ruefully and said, "Let's go back. You still look as wary as some captured creature—ready to leap at the slightest sign of danger. Maybe I can eventually convince you that the bonds aren't all that bad."

She made an effort to sound normal. "You lead the way."

The trip back down the grassy hillside was quiet. As the track widened, Grant lengthened his stride and Jean moved up to walk alongside. Both were content to enjoy the sunshine and silence; both equally loath to disturb it.

When they arrived back at the cabin, Jean hesitated on the step.

"Are you coming back to the house?" she asked uncertainly, not sure whether he would take offense at the question.

"I guess so." Grant shifted the hamper so that he could look at his watch. "Let's put this stuff away first and then I'll lock up here."

"I can do that." She went ahead of him to open the door. "There isn't much to unpack."

"Then give me about five minutes to get changed," he said casually. "We might go out after dinner and see if we can find a place for dancing."

"That would be nice. I think Ernie said the Inn had a new combo this week."

"Fine." He paused on the stairs leading up to the bedroom and looked down on her. "Let's keep it quiet, though. Otherwise we'll end up on that double date with Toby and Doreen."

"Is that bad?"

He shook his head impatiently. "You know what I mean. Let them make their own plans."

"Whatever you say." She watched him take the stairs two at a time with a light in her eyes. "I'll start disposing of the remains. It's a good thing you have garbage collection now or I'd have to start digging a hole."

His muffled laugh drifted down. "The blanket goes on the same shelf in the hall closet as the hamper, in case you're wondering."

"I'll find it," she called up to him, "and if I have any other questions I'll ask Homer."

She hummed softly as she unpacked the remnants of picnic fare and stored leftover potato salad in the refrigerator. The Thermos was rinsed and left to drain by the sink while she disposed of the paper plates and plastic cutlery. Finally, when everything was in its place, she replaced the lid on the wicker hamper and went down the hall to store it away.

There was a conveniently empty space on the top shelf in the closet and she tried to shove the basket onto it but it stuck halfway. Puzzled, she pulled it back out and reached up to find the obstruction. Her groping fingers encountered a zipper airline bag wedged at the back of the shelf and she pulled it out so that she could put the picnic hamper in its place. Once she

120

had accomplished that, she started to shift the small bag onto a lower shelf, when she noted part of its contents spilling out of the open top.

Still holding the bag, she reached over to turn on the closet light. The additional illumination merely served to confirm her suspicions.

In an almost trancelike state, she emptied the bag and surveyed the contents. There were three pieces of the most feminine apparel—a cocoa-colored lace bikini bra and brief set lined with opaque chiffon and an unlined hip-hugging jacket of the same lace. A matching satin ribbon edged the coat at the bosom creating a deep V-shaped decolleté. Whether the pieces were designed for sunning, swimming, or sleeping, it was the most seductive outfit Jean had ever seen. Evidently Grant thought so too or he wouldn't have let his girlfriend keep them around.

She bit the inner flesh of her lip as she recalled his recent protestation of innocence and wondered what his glib answer would be for this. No doubt he'd have one!

Angrily she stuffed the lingerie back into the bag and shoved it onto an empty place on the shelf. Then she let herself out the back door of the cottage without a backward glance. This time there were no regrets—she couldn't get away fast enough.

She was some fifty feet up the roadway when she heard a hail and Grant's feet pounding on the dirt behind her.

He caught her arm and spun her around. "What in the devil do you think you're doing? I saw you from the upper window." He was breathing hard and his unbuttoned dress shirt was hanging over his trousers.

She yanked her elbow away. "Then you must have seen that I was on my way home."

He was still puzzled. "There's no need to walk. I'll be ready to go in a few minutes and we'll take the car."

"*You* can take the car anywhere you want to." Her words came out like carefully spaced icicles. "I am going to walk. Alone . . ." she added pointedly, "from now on."

"I see." A grimness settled over his face. "Would it do any good to ask what brought on this latest temper tantrum of yours?"

"I don't owe you anything . . . least of all any more explanations."

"Back to the cold front, eh?"

"Call it anything you damn well like," she shouted, trying to keep from breaking into tears in front of him. "I'm sick of having you yank my feelings around like a yo-yo. Do me a favor and stay as far away as possible from now on. This time I mean it."

His eyes glittered with fury. "I'll be happy to oblige, lady. Your friend Bart can suspect what he pleases and you can make whatever explanations you like to the others."

"What do you want me to tell them . . ."

He interrupted callously. "Tell them we have a modern marriage. We don't let anything interfere with our private lives."

Belatedly the contents of that zipper bag flashed in her mind and she snapped, "That's been evident all along. Marriage vows didn't cramp your style in the least."

He had turned toward the cottage, but whirled around at her last taunt. "I don't know what in the hell you're talking about." The words were uttered in a dangerous soft tone. "And I doubt if you do. But since you already seem to know such a lot about my love life . . ." he reached over and yanked her figure hard against his tall form, "you might as well get a few of the side benefits."

Before she could pull back in surprise, he lowered his head and parted her lips in a long and ruthless kiss.

Jean's amazement changed rapidly to anger which gradually made way for a totally different feeling as the embrace continued. The net result was too provocative to bear analyzing just then.

When he finally released her, she sagged and clutched

at his arm to keep from falling. Intense emotion left her speechless; not so with Grant.

"Now—go home and sleep tight, Mrs. Stevenson," he snarled. "Don't worry about dragging out that black sweater unless you want to keep warm. You can damn well bet on having that cold bed all to yourself from now on."

He swung on his heel and strode off toward the cottage.

It was only feminine pride that allowed Jean to get up around the curve in the road and out of sight before she sank down on a convenient rock. She scrubbed helplessly at her bruised lips with the back of her hand but there was no erasing of the memory.

Certainly she wasn't going to cry. Not over such an arrogant, hateful, scheming, deceitful . . . Her list of adjectives ran out and she concentrated on searching for a handkerchief to blow her nose hard. As she mopped her wet cheeks and eyes, she assured herself it was merely an allergy . . . nothing more.

She sat there for quite a time.

But she didn't need long to decide that for a woman who had only recently started to make a mess of her life—she was doing a remarkably thorough job of it.

Chapter *EIGHT*

Jean watched the weekend drag past and felt like a prisoner reduced to marking off the days on a calendar.

It was useless to blame her lethargy on the weather. The elements performed miracles for the season with the south breeze as gentle as a baby's breath and the sunshine flaunting itself at all hours.

In the midst of it all, Jean wandered back and forth on the beach like a desolate Crusoe feeling as forsaken and out-of-place as a vegetarian at a steak dinner.

Doreen had driven off to spend some time with a college friend in Portland. Before she left, she informed Jean that Toby was taking part in a golf tournament at a resort down the coast and that Bart had gone along to kibitz. At noon, Mrs. Lloyd called to say she was going clamming on the Washington beach for a few days if Jean didn't mind. Naturally Jean didn't.

The main character in the drama was missing too. If Grant stirred out of his cottage, he didn't do it during Jean's two hurried trips to the Sea Bend supermarket. Each time she drove by she inspected the parking lot carefully before turning in to the store. The possibility of a chance encounter while selecting ripe tomatoes or a custard pie was too horrible to contemplate.

One day she saw Rick in the distance and received a cheery wave; the next afternoon she merely caught a flash of red paint as his bicycle disappeared up the road. By Monday morning, she was down to wishing that Homer and his pickle jar were around for companionship. A few minutes later, after hearing the Scottish lament "Will Ye No Come Back Again" on the radio and breaking into tears, she decided to take herself to task.

"Snap out of it," she muttered to herself as she carried a mug of coffee out to the patio and stood staring through the glass barrier at the midmorning sunlight sparkling on the breakers below. After all, now that she was married and had her inheritance, there was no need for her to spend any more lonely days at Sea Bend. She could go back to her job in New Orleans . . . and be lonely there. "Damn him!" she said loudly and emptied her coffee mug over an unsuspecting clematis.

"Try another cupful," Toby said behind her, "you missed a couple leaves."

Jean whirled. "Toby! You startled me—I didn't hear your car."

"That's because I left it down on the road. I was checking the beach stairs and it was such a nice morning I decided to walk up and scrounge a cup of coffee. Is there any left or did you water the rest of the garden before I came?"

"That was the only plant. I was thinking of something else."

"So I gathered. Should I ask who you were mentally consigning to the devil?"

"Not if you want any of my coffee."

"That's what I thought. I'll take the coffee, thanks." He pulled up a rattan chair. "You don't mind if I sit out here and stay out of range, do you?"

She paused on the kitchen step. "By all means—

but are you sure you can trust me with hot liquid?"

Toby merely closed his eyes.

Five minutes later, she plonked a tray down on the table in front of him.

"Your coffee, sahib."

He kept his eyes closed. "No dancing girls?" There was an ominous silence and he hastily opened them. "Hey—bring that tray back. I'm starving."

Obediently she changed course. "You're always starving. How was the golf tournament?"

"So so. I was hooking too much on the second nine, but it wasn't bad."

"Which means you brought home another plaque."

"You can read all about it when the local rag comes out next week." He took a sip of coffee and reached over for the plate of homemade doughnuts. "I was hoping for some of these. When is Doreen coming back?"

"Sometime today." Jean broke a doughnut in half and nibbled on it. "She said it wouldn't be late."

"How about the four of us going out to dinner tonight? Grant should be back by then. His plane gets in to Portland about three, doesn't it?"

She stared at him blankly.

He looked up from his plate to meet her gaze. "Doesn't that nonstop flight from Los Angeles get in at three-fifteen?"

"I'm not sure of the new schedule," she stalled, deciding she needed time to think. Abruptly she pushed back from the table and went over to donate her crumbled doughnut to an inquisitive sparrow.

So Grant had been away in Los Angeles and she had holed up like a mole fearing that he was just over the hill. All the subterfuge had been an utter waste of time. She decided wearily that most everything she did lately fitted in that category.

"Are you going to meet him?" Toby's voice finally penetrated.

"Who?"

"My God! Grant, of course. What's the matter with

126

you? I find you talking to yourself—sloshing coffee over the greenery. . . ."

"It's good for the soil," she said feebly. "I read about it somewhere."

"Then read the rest of the paragraph, idiot. They were talking about coffee grounds. All you did was give the vine insomnia." As if the word tripped a mental key, he automatically reached over and re-filled his coffee cup before continuing. "Now you can't even remember who you're supposed to meet at the airport."

"I know who I'm supposed to, but I'm not going to."

"The community college has an 'English for Im-migrants' class this quarter. . . . I'll put you down for it."

"Go to the dickens!" she flared. "I can't think how Doreen stands having you around."

"It's my easygoing personality . . . unlike some people I could mention these days." He bestowed a complacent smirk upon her before returning to the inquisition. "Why aren't you going to meet Grant?"

"Why don't you . . ."

"Ah, ah . . ."

"Mind your own concerns," she finished weakly.

"I am. I have a proprietary interest in you," he said calmly. "You have a piece of land that I want and besides you were my girl first."

"You may get the land after all," she said, ignoring his latter statement. "Now that conditions have changed and I don't have to live here any longer to inherit—I'm going back to New Orleans."

He frowned. "You must be more addlepated than I thought. New Orleans won't suit Grant at all. He has a damn good job in Los Angeles and I can't see him leaving it to follow his rich wife around."

Jean started to tell him that this was precisely why she was planning on Louisiana and then thought better of it. "We haven't made any definite plans," she admitted finally.

"Well, don't go tearing off until we get this plant

question settled," he warned. "You haven't heard the latest. Bart told me over the weekend that Foster has resigned, so now we have to hunt for a new manager."

"But Mr. Foster has been there for ages . . ." her voice rose in astonishment. "Why would he resign now just a few years before retirement?"

"The official reason was ill health, but Bart was pretty unhappy about it. He claims there isn't anyone good enough to take Foster's place. Now he's talking about bring someone up from his California organization."

"What do you think of that?"

"I'm not sure. It all depends on what Grant says."

She gave him a puzzled look. "That isn't like you. You're relying on his judgment a great deal these days."

"Wouldn't you—after hearing him tell about the plywood industry potential. There's no doubt that Bart painted the wrong sales picture."

"What did he say when you asked him about it?"

"Not much . . . merely pointed out that we hadn't been able to land many contracts."

"Maybe he shifted the blame to Foster and that's why he resigned."

"It's possible. We'll wait and see. You know, Jean— if you and Grant polled your voting stock along with mine, we could move Bart right out of the driver's seat." He stopped her protest by continuing, "I'm not saying that it's a good idea—yet. Bart has a tremendous reputation for making money. Let's wait and see what he comes up with this time."

"Whatever you like. Frankly, I'm sick of the whole thing."

"Evidently that's not the only trouble. You look like an unhappy spaniel today. What's the matter, Jeanie?" There was genuine concern in his eyes.

She shook her head wordlessly.

He finished the last swallow of coffee and stood up. "Well, come on out to dinner tonight and try a therapeutic champagne cocktail. Ernie puts in all the right ingredients." He pulled her to him in an awkward hug. "I'll check with you later on. Ask Doreen to give me a ring when she arrives—I'll be at the office."

"I'll tell her," she promised, "but don't count on me for dinner."

"Nonsense. You and Grant can postpone your cozy twosomes until later on."

"Don't be funny."

"What's funny about a honeymoon couple wanting to spend some time alone?" He pursed his lips thoughtfully. "Though I'm damned if I know why I'm defending the married state to you. If Grant's absence has this effect on you, there must be more to matrimony than I thought."

She shooed him toward the drive. "When I want a psychiatrist, I'll call for an appointment. Until then—do me a favor and stop asking questions. Next you'll be requesting a testimonial."

His grin was wicked. "You're a little mixed-up. Grant's the one I'd ask for that."

"*Good-bye,* Toby."

"All right, I'm going. I know when I'm not wanted. At least, Doreen appreciates me."

"Then I'd wrap her up and take her home." Jean's voice was light, but her blue eyes were completely serious.

"I'll keep it in mind," he said after a moment's thought and turned to saunter down the drive.

Five minutes later, he looked down to see the convertible Doreen had been using for her weekend parked next to his car in a scenic view area by the road.

His steps quickened, but when he arrived at the cars he found both of them deserted and no sign of the decorative redhead. Leaning on the horn in his car he gave two long blasts and then called her name.

Her answering hail came immediately.

"Where the devil are you?" he persisted, looking around in bewilderment.

"Halfway down the cliff," she bleated, "hanging on by my clenched fingertips."

He moved rapidly but cautiously beyond the barrier and peered over the sandy edge. Doreen was about seven feet from the top huddled at the back of a narrow ledge.

"What in God's name are you doing down there?" The overwhelming sense of relief he felt didn't escape him.

"Admiring the view," she said sweetly, too sweetly, "but I'm finished now and I'd like to come up."

"That can be arranged. I'll come down and boost you. . . ."

"No!" Her voice was sharp. "Don't come close to that edge. I tried scrambling up but the sand gives way."

"Okay—hold tight. There's some rope in the trunk of my car." He peered at her anxiously. "Can you manage that? I mean, you aren't hurt, are you?"

"Only my pride. Get the rope. I'm scared to breathe deeply in case this ledge gives way."

Toby set a new speed record for getting to his car and back. He snaked over a double thickness of tough dacron line saying, "Knot that carefully under your arms and then hang on like crazy. When you're ready —I'll stand well back and pull."

"Okay," she agreed breathlessly. Then in a minute or two: "Let's go."

It took only seconds before her disheveled figure stumbled over the edge and she was pulled into his protective embrace.

"All right?" he asked, looking anxiously down into her dirty face.

She nodded—not trusting her voice right then.

"Then what were you thinking of scrambling over cliff tops?" he said crossly in a surge of relief at having her safe and sound. "You shouldn't have gone beyond the barrier in the first place."

"I know." For Doreen the words were abnormally meek. "But it's really all your fault."

"Mine!"

She nodded again. "I saw your car and decided you must be nearby so I stopped to talk to you. While I was wandering around trying to find you, I thought I heard voices down on the beach so I went to the cliff edge

130

and peeked over. Then the part under my feet started crumbling and the next thing I knew I had slithered down onto that ledge." She made an unhappy grimace as she looked at her scratched hands. "My nails won't be the same for months—I was scrabbling like a badger trying to stop myself."

"Be thankful your neck is still the same. If the ledge had crumpled . . ."

"I know." She shuddered. "Don't tell me any more about the beauty of your isolated beach. I just stood there praying that someone would come."

"Shhh." He pulled her close again. "Everything's okay now. I'm not sure that it's safe to let you run around loose though."

"Who'd volunteer to keep me in order?" Her voice was just a thread of sound against his shoulder.

"I think I might," he said slowly, as if amazed at his own words. "That's if you agree it's a good idea."

Her face was radiant when she looked up. "Toby! Do you mean it?"

"Damned if I don't. Seeing you in danger made the bottom drop right out of my world."

"You're confused," she said impishly, caressing the back of his head. "We were worried about the bottom dropping out of my world."

"Then remind me," he drawled as he tilted up her chin, "to give you lessons in climbing."

"Some other time, darling," her lips smiled invitingly, "some other time."

The kiss was infinitely satisfying to both of them and they spent the next few minutes discovering that repetition increased the enjoyment. It took the raucous sound of an automobile horn on the road beside them to make them spring apart.

"Who the . . . ?" Toby exclaimed irritably and then broke into a grin and waved at the departing motorist. He turned back to Doreen and explained. "Ernie. That saves us the trouble of sending an announcement to the paper."

"Not on your life." She tucked her arm lightly through his. "We'll tell the papers and I may even

131

shout it from a few rooftops. The only way you could escape now, Toby Calhoun, would be to hijack a plane to Cuba."

"You don't have to worry, my sweet. You have infinitely more appeal than Fidel. Come on . . ." he pulled her toward the car. "Let's go tell my relatives."

"And Bart too." She smiled. "Won't he have a fit! Right after the shock of Jean and Grant's marriage." Her expression sobered immediately. "This isn't something on the rebound for me, Toby. I thought Grant was terrific, but there was never anything serious between us." Then she added painstakingly, "Not that I should take any credit for that state of affairs—it was all Grant's doing."

"That makes two of us," he agreed wryly. "Don't forget, I was in the same position with Jean."

"Were you in love with her?"

"I thought I was." The words came out slowly. "But the way I felt then couldn't hold a candle to the way I'm feeling now, so Jean was right all along. She claimed we weren't in love." He grinned as he stopped to search for his car key. "Now I know what she meant."

"Ummm—you can say that again." Doreen stopped by the car door. "I wonder," she said dreamily, "why we've just discovered this blissful state? We've been stumbling over each other for years."

"You didn't fall off a cliff before."

She slid onto the front seat. "Well, I'm glad it convinced you because frankly I don't intend to do it again."

It was almost dinner-time when Doreen finally arrived at the house.

Jean watched her drive up and met her at the front door. "I was about to send out the bloodhounds," she told her.

Doreen enveloped her in an enthusiastic hug. "I've never been less lost in my entire life—if that makes sense!" She whirled ecstatically around in the hall. "Oh Jean . . . it really happened! We even told his mother and she couldn't have been sweeter. I don't have a ring yet, but he wants to get one out of the safe deposit box, so I should have it tomorrow."

"Wait a minute—you're going too fast for me. Take it a step at a time. Is this someone you met in Portland?"

Doreen wrinkled her nose. "Of course not. It's Toby. T-O-B-Y. I met him earlier today when he pulled me up the cliff and . . ."

"He did what?"

"Got me off a ledge. I'll tell you about that later. The only important thing is that we're engaged. Honest, truly, really family-approved engaged."

"Dorrie, that's wonderful!" Jean's face lit up with genuine delight. "I'm so happy for both of you. Have you told Bart?"

"No—darn it. I tried to, but he wasn't in the office so I left a message for him to call." Doreen's forehead creased in a faint frown. "He won't be happy, but there isn't much he can do about it. After all, I am of age and other than serving as my investment advisor, he hasn't any legal control."

"But why wouldn't he approve of Toby? I'd think he'd have everything a girl's family could want."

"I think so myself," Doreen said complacently, "but Uncle Bart doesn't like to have anything all signed, sealed, and delivered. I'd hate to hurt him because he's family, but it seems to me that he gets more crotchety and unreasonable all the time."

"Well, don't fuss before you have to," Jean advised. "What are your plans for dinner?"

Doreen stretched out on the davenport and pulled a cushion under her head. "I don't know. Toby said he'd call a little later. He's still trying to get in touch with Grant. Did he call you from the airport?"

"Not that I know of. I was outside gardening most of the afternoon so I may have missed the phone." A stern inner voice reminded her that she was at the very bottom of Grant's telephone list and completely off his visiting list. She sighed and edged toward the kitchen. "You and Toby had better plan a private celebration tonight and I'll take a casserole out of the freezer."

"Why don't you hold off until we hear from Grant?"

"There's no point in it. He'll probably be tired after his flight. We'll still have time to give you a proper party before I leave."

Doreen looked up round-eyed. "Leave? Where on earth are you going?"

"New Orleans. There are some loose ends I should take care of." She added hastily, "I hope you'll stay on here. Mrs. Lloyd will be delighted to look after you."

"But what about Grant? Or will he go with you?"

Jean concentrated on adjusting the waistband of her skirt and kept her voice without expression. "I doubt if he can fit it into his schedule. He'd rather stay in the cottage, I'm sure."

"He does have a passion for the place." Doreen's tone carefully followed suit, but there was nothing casual about the glance she bestowed on Jean. "Toby hoped you might talk him into staying on at the plant."

"But Grant's a chemist. . . ."

"He's also a darned good businessman. I know Bart didn't plan to use him strictly in a lab when he offered him a job in California. If you could persuade him to stay in Sea Bend, think what a fine time the four of us could have."

Jean looked hurriedly away so that Doreen wouldn't notice the unhappiness her words caused. It was heartrending to even think of leading a normal married life with Grant in such a beautiful place. By comparison, trudging to her job each day and living in a career-girl apartment in New Orleans was hard to contemplate.

"Wouldn't that be fun?" Doreen was insistent.

Jean came back to normal. "Yes—but not very practical, I'm afraid. I'd better get that casserole in the oven."

"I'll keep you company and make a cup of coffee," Doreen said, getting up and following her out to the kitchen. She watched Jean check the contents of the

134

freezer. "Don't you dare disappear back to New Orleans until I get my wedding date fixed. You're positively the only person I'll accept as matron of honor."

Jean pulled out a foil-wrapped dish and closed the freezer door with her hip. "I accept with pleasure," she said definitely. "Don't worry, I'd come from further than Louisiana for you and Toby."

"I still hope you'll be here at Sea Bend." Doreen filled a copper kettle and perched on a kitchen stool while she waited for the water to boil. "Toby took me to look at a view lot of his before he brought me home. He thought it would be a good place for us to build."

Jean made an impudent face. "You can't fool me—your fiancé was finally able to combine his true loves."

Doreen nodded in response. "You know Toby and real estate. It's his favorite occupation. Besides, he *is* the possessive type. I had an inkling down at Grant's cottage last week."

"Toby was laying down the law?"

The other shrugged wryly. "We stopped off to see Grant before Toby took me on for a swim at the Club. I couldn't wait to display my new bikini set. . . ."

Jean felt an icy sensation spread over her. "Was it cocoa-colored lace with a matching jacket?" she asked.

"That's the one. Anyhow, I dragged it out of the bag to show them and Toby flatly refused to let me appear at the pool in it. He said it might be fine for the Riviera, but he wasn't going to have half of Sea Bend ogling and the other half talking about me. So I poked it back in the bag and we played golf instead." She reached over to measure instant coffee in a cup and poured boiling water over it. "I must pick it up one of these days—if it's still down there."

"It's still there," Jean said, shoving her casserole in the oven and, with difficulty, resisting the urge to shove her head in alongside. "Left-hand side of the shelf in the hall closet."

"Did Grant show it to you? He had a fit too."

"I was the one who had the fit this time. He didn't know I saw it." Jean decided to put her cards on the

135

table because they were too heavy to hold any longer. "You see, I didn't know the bikini belonged to you. It was scarcely decent," she put in defensively.

Doreen ignored the last comment. "And you thought it belonged to one of Grant's lady loves?" Her voice rose incredulously. "Jean—you fool! Grant isn't that kind."

"All men are that kind if they have the chance."

"Well, look at it this way. Grant certainly wouldn't be keeping evidence like that when he's married. He kept miles away from any kind of involvement even when he was single—and I know." She took a sip of coffee. "Wasn't he curious as to why you were mad?"

"I didn't give him a chance. I just said something idiotic like never darkening my door again."

"And?"

Jean shook her head hopelessly. "He hasn't."

Doreen nodded in sympathy. "Men are the very devil for taking a woman at her word and it really isn't fair. Especially when most women have completely changed their minds a half hour later." She took another sip of coffee and said, "I was afraid something was wrong but when I heard about the business trip to California, I decided I was imagining things."

"You weren't. He didn't tell me he was going and I know darned well he won't report in when he gets back. This time he's *really* mad."

"Maybe you're taking it too seriously. Bridegrooms can find a way around their problems."

"Yes, but . . ." Jean started to say that Grant wasn't the usual type of bridegroom and stopped. She couldn't bear to tell anyone the truth about that forced marriage—where the promises to love and cherish weren't valid even though the ceremony was.

"But what?" Doreen asked.

"Nothing." Jean made a project out of setting the oven thermostat. "I'm sorry to have unloaded all this on you."

"That's what friends are for. That . . . and giving advice."

Jean took refuge behind the kitchen table.

"Absence won't make the heart grow fonder in this case," Doreen continued, "so I'd skip New Orleans. Apologies are the order of the day since you raised the ruckus."

"I . . . just . . . couldn't."

"You'd better. It's a case of sink your pride or your marriage. You know what I said about women changing their minds . . . well, men don't. Not when they've been unjustly accused—not one iota of a budge." She took a spoon and flicked a minute foreign substance from the top of her coffee. "I'm afraid, Jeanie gal, you'd better start practicing apologies because . . ."

"Because?"

Doreen set her cup down with a bang. "Because it's a cinch that Grant won't."

Chapter NINE

⎯⎯⎯➤◆◆◆◆⎯⎯⎯

The next development came from an unexpected source.

Jean was returning from volunteer duty at the hospital the following afternoon when she was hailed by a sharp childish voice as she neared her front door.

"Hi . . . Mrs. Stevenson . . . wait up!" Rick dog-trotted up the drive and waved a white envelope to attract her attention. "I have something for you."

"Take it easy," Jean called and waited on the step. "You shouldn't have hurried so," she scolded as he pulled up beside her, breathing hard.

"I thought this might be important." He thrust the envelope in her hand and they both stared down at it. "Some guy put it in your paper box right after you zipped up the drive. He must have figured you'd see it when you came down to get the paper."

Jean tapped the envelope against her thumbnail and tried to ignore the apprehensive feeling connected with her name on the outside of it. She glanced at Rick. "Then you saw the man . . . did you recognize him?"

"Nah." He sounded disgusted with himself. "He moved too fast. It was just somebody with work

138

clothes on—sort of average-looking. I didn't know it was important," he added plaintively.

"It probably isn't."

"I can tell you one thing though. It was a company pickup he was driving."

To Sea Bend residents, the plywood plant was the only "company" in town and Jean's frown became more pronounced. Evidently her feeling of foreboding was justified; any normal messages from the plant came by telephone or occasionally on official stationery—not in a smudged envelope with her name printed untidily on the front of it.

"Well, Mrs. Stevenson, I'd better keep goin' with my route."

"Of course, Rick. Thank you very much for bringing this up." She managed a creditable smile despite her inner qualms. "How is Max these days?"

"Great! I moved him into his new cage today and now the principal is talking about taking him around to some of the other schools in the county as sort of a traveling exhibit." He grinned proudly. "He says it isn't everybody that has a four-foot iguana."

"That's certainly true."

"You're going to come down and see him in his new house, aren't you? Mr. Stevenson said you would."

"Absolutely. Let me know when it's convenient."

"My science teacher plans to hold an official house-warming. He says you and Mr. Stevenson will get the first invitation."

She tousled his hair affectionately. "Do we send flowers to Max?" she teased.

"Better not. He'll just eat them."

"Then we'll make it a nosegay of carrots surrounded by lettuce leaves. Get along now or you'll be late."

"Okay. I'll see 'ya tomorrow." He gave a cheerful wave and scurried back down the drive.

Jean's smile faded as soon as he disappeared from sight. She looked again at the envelope in her hand and then walked slowly into the house, grateful that she could study its contents in private.

139

She wasn't long in finding out what they were. The note was typewritten and mercifully short:

If you want to keep Grant Stevenson healthy, come to the steam room in the plant at eleven o'clock tonight and bring five thousand dollars in small bills. Come alone and stay away from the police.

There was no signature at the bottom of the note to help identify the writer.

Jean looked at her watch. Five o'clock. Evidently whoever delivered the letter knew that the drive-in window of the bank stayed open until six. There was still time to collect the money if it was necessary.

She shook her head despairingly. Was it necessary? Could Grant be in actual danger now—was that why she hadn't heard from him?

The feminine pride she had been nursing took an abrupt tumble as she reached for her car keys and swung back to the door. Obviously the first thing to do was check the cottage.

Although she probably set a new speed record for getting there, she could tell the cabin was deserted as soon as she drove up. The chimney was not smoking and the curtains shrouding the long windows were tightly pulled. Even so, it was impossible to tell whether Grant had departed days or merely hours ago.

Jean thought of leaving a note on the front door and then abandoned the idea. It was one thing to scrawl "Back in a few minutes" on a piece of paper and yet another to write "Your life is in danger—please call me at your convenience." Grant would call the authorities all right, but most likely the ones in white coats who would then come calling on her.

Reluctantly she turned the car and drove slowly back toward the highway. If Grant wasn't available, who could she call? Despite the warning in the note, she wasn't rash enough to march off into the darkness without letting someone know where she was going.

Doreen and Toby were the obvious ones, but they

140

had driven down the coast earlier in the day. She could leave a note in case they returned before midnight, but it was difficult to know what to say. There just wasn't an easy way to write "If I'm not back by one o'clock in the morning, send out the State Patrol!"

She sneaked a glance at her watch. Five-fifteen. If she was going to get the money, she'd better do it now.

At the junction, she turned right toward town. She drove automatically, her mind busy with other things. It was fortunate that she had five thousand dollars in her checking account . . . providential that a stock dividend from the estate had just been deposited. Thinking it over, she decided it was almost too providential. She mentally listed the people who could have known about the payment and then threw the list out the window. There was no reason to believe her suspicions were valid along that line.

If only Grant had stopped being so stubborn and informed her of his whereabouts. If she knew whether he was back from California. If—if—if. The word flashed over and over in her mind. It was inconceivable to think of his being in trouble or held against his will. Yet even the remote possibility made her feel frozen with misery.

The transaction at the bank was short and blessedly the teller exhibited no curiosity at the sizable withdrawal. As Jean drove off she was grateful that her connection with the plant made dealing with such a sum plausible. The teller probably thought the money was connected with payroll or taxes.

She recognized Toby's secretary in the car directly behind hers. Evidently she did her banking at the last possible moment as well. They exchanged a wave of recognition and then Jean concentrated on her driving.

On an impulse she turned the car toward the Inn. There was a chance that Grant would be dining there; she could give him the letter and coolly ask his advice. Then sometime during the evening she would find a way to apologize for her outburst the last time they had been together.

141

She was still in a pleasant make-believe world that had Grant back to his friendly self and inviting her to rescue him from a lonely evening when she parked at the Inn. From then on, reality took over.

If Grant was around, he took care to stay out of sight. In the dimly lit lounge, Ernie's stocky figure was gone from its familiar place behind the bar. When she asked the reception clerk if Mr. Winthrop were available, she was told politely that he was out and had left no word concerning his return. If she would care to leave a message. . . .

Jean shook her head slowly and trudged back to the car. Generally the Inn thronged with acquaintances. Why was it that when a person wanted to see a familiar face there was an absolute drought. Evidently there was nothing for it except to go home and wait for eleven o'clock to come.

The evening dragged interminably.

By nine o'clock she felt as neglected as Homer in his lonely pickle jar. Doreen and Toby persisted in remaining stubbornly among the missing. When she called the Inn at ten and asked for Mr. Winthrop, she was told that he was still out. On asking for Mr. Stevenson to be paged, she struck out again. After the operator said there was no answer, she thanked her and then banged the receiver down so hard that she caught her finger under the headrest. She blinked back tears and knew they were from frustration rather than pain. So, turning from the phone, she chewed on the bruised knuckle and solemnly faced facts.

If every person she knew remained out of reach, she'd manage on her own without any help. After all, she had existed for quite a few years without assistance. Her decision left her feeling more depressed than ever and she trudged down the hall into her bedroom to change her clothes, wondering what an idiot wore when she paid blackmail money.

Something warm if she was expected to lurk in dark corners. Something dark if she went by the last television movie featuring a cat burglar.

She pulled out some dark-gray slacks and a long-

142

sleeved slate-blue shirt. That combination together with a navy-blue pea jacket should fit all qualifications.

The money was more difficult. Even in twenties and tens, it wasn't easy to compress five thousand dollars into a small package. Finally, she pulled a generous over-the-shoulder bag from her closet and stuffed the bills into it. Her unknown letter-writer could find his own way to carry it home.

She set out from the house at ten-thirty. The only message she left for Doreen was a brief note saying that she was going to the plant and should be back by midnight. With any luck, she could collect Grant and return before Doreen came in from her date.

She drove carefully down the drive and out onto the main highway without encountering more than an occasional car. Sea Bend social life tended to dissolve about ten o'clock except for an unusual weekend or holiday when the natives stayed up until midnight.

She flicked on her bright lights when it was time for the plant turnoff and felt a shiver of trepidation as she pulled the car onto the side road. For the first time since she had left the house, the course to which she had committed herself seemed foolhardy in the extreme. She swallowed with an effort and concluded it was too late for dithering.

The car idled along the road and she scanned the parking lot adjacent to the business offices. It was deserted except for a modest utility truck in a far corner which probably belonged to a guard. Certain key employees would report for the swing shift at two o'clock, but the bulk of personnel wouldn't come in until eight in the morning.

She drove into the lot and parked by the wire fence next to the road. Then she checked her watch in the light of the dashboard. Right on time. That meant the letter writer was probably keeping her under observation at this very moment.

The slamming of her car door echoed loud in the stillness of the night and she stood motionless for a moment—as skittish as a cat in unfamiliar territory. Only the thought of Grant's possible danger stiffened her resolve and made her walk slowly toward the plywood plant entrance.

The front door didn't creak as she crept through, but to her keyed-up senses, the high-ceilinged building was fraught with sinister hiding places. Illumination was provided by small bulbs at irregular intervals. Enough to allow the watchman to make his rounds without stumbling but not enough to eliminate shadowy valleys behind the towering piles of plywood.

A sudden creak at the far side of the building made her start nervously, but it was immediately followed by the whirr of an electric motor and she continued down the middle of an aisle. Her echoing footsteps went past the deserted sanders and the half-full sorting bins. Overhead the stilled conveyor belt looked like a grotesque study in arrested motion.

Heat still emanated from the big drying oven and she hurried past it, staying as far away as possible. Her steps slowed again as she approached the monstrous peeler with its chain grips hanging ominously in the gloom. The sharp points which impaled giant logs looked dangerous even as they dangled motionlessly.

Jean felt a thudding in her ears and became aware of her rapid heartbeat. Her sense of dread was so great that when a muffled weight fell in the corner behind her, she was almost lightheaded with relief. For a moment there was complete silence and then the barest rustle of movement marked the source. Jean turned in a half-circle and moved inexorably toward it.

The sight of a masculine figure sprawled on the floor by a rough wooden bin made her gasp and dart forward. She was whimpering wordlessly as she tugged to get it out of the shadow.

"Take it easy, lady. There's no sense in movin' him."

The masculine voice behind her made Jean leap to her feet and spin around in terror.

A stocky middle-aged man in grimy work clothes lounged against a nearby forklift. "I told 'ya not to bring anybody," he complained.

"But I didn't bring anyone!" Her feeling of panic

144

subsided slightly at that accusation. "I followed your instructions exactly." She knelt once again by the fallen figure. "We have to move him into the light and send for a doctor. . . ."

"Leave him alone!" the other instructed. "We're not calling anybody in until we transact our business."

"But you promised not to hurt my husband."

"Stevenson's okay and he'll stay that way—if you brought the money."

Jean's eyes rounded in wonder at his remark and then she reached over to tug the unconscious figure into a pool of light. "Ernie!" She stared up at the lounging figure. "What's he doing here?"

He shrugged. "Play it any way you like, lady. He's out for the count now."

"But I didn't bring him. . . ."

"Then why was his car practically on your back bumper when you drove in the yard? It took me all this time to get the drop on him. I told you I didn't want company." His glance swept over her. "Where's the money?"

"It's nearby," Jean stalled, glad that she had left her bag in the trunk of the car.

"That's not good enough. I know you went to the bank—I was watching."

She straightened her shoulders. "Then you must know that I'm not going to hand it over until I find out about my husband."

He laughed. It was a nasty wheeze that destroyed most of Jean's self-control.

"I like your nerve, doll." For a moment, the look he bestowed was of a completely different type.

"Don't call me that," she said sharply. Unconsciously she stepped backward. "What kind of information do you have to sell that's worth five thousand dollars?"

"Silence. Pure, golden, silence—to keep your husband out of the clink. I was working in that plant of his in California when the explosion took place. The police want a witness who can tell them what really happened."

"Grant didn't do anything. . . ."

145

"Didn't he? That could be hard to prove—especially against the word of a disinterested party."

"Who'd believe your word against Grant's?"

"Plenty of people," he smirked. "Especially when they hear that Bart Winthrop recommended me for the job." He noted her amazed look with satisfaction. "I thought that would throw you. There's no sense in stirrin' up trouble. I'm willing to forget lots of things and right now I want to move on." He ran a nervous tongue over his lips. "That takes money. Five thousand will get me to where I want to go. You won't hear from me again."

She pushed her hair back from her face. "You're going too fast. What guarantee do I have that you'd keep your word?"

"Lady, you're in no position to ask for guarantees."

"You're forgetting that I have the five thousand dollars."

"I'm not forgetting anything, but you are." He jerked his head toward Ernie's silent and crumpled figure. "Let's cut the conversation and I'll be on my way. Where's the money?"

Jean took a deep breath. "You can threaten all you want. I'm not paying anything until I find out where my husband is."

"My gawd—is that all." He wiped a grimy hand under his nose. "He's tucked away nice and neat in that cottage of his. I'd let you phone him except that I had to leave him tied up. There wasn't anybody to watch over him." He smirked again. "Nobody else for you to pay off, so you can hand over the money and I'll go. Even Stevenson knows that I work alone."

"You mean my husband knows you?"

"He does now."

She scowled fiercely. "He said something about a man looking familiar. It was when we visited the plant." Her expression cleared. "*You* were the man we saw by the car. When we were driving away, Grant said . . ." Her voice trailed off and then came back in a spurt of anger. "Driving! It was right after we

146

saw you that I had trouble with the car. You were the one who tampered with the brakes!"

"I wondered when you'd get 'round to that."

"So that's why you have to leave town. . . ."

"Hell no, lady." He was completely disgusted. "You can yap all you want about the brakes on that car, but you can't prove a thing."

"Then why?"

"Cut the talk. It's getting late and I want to vamoose. Let's have the money."

"I don't have it with me . . ." she broke off as Ernie stirred slightly. "You can't leave him here. He needs medical attention."

"I can't get through to you that you'll need medical attention too unless you hand over that money."

Her pale face turned even whiter. "Why should I pay you? You're lying about Grant—you're probably lying about everything!" Her glance flicked desperately toward the open corridor behind him. If only she could get past to find help.

He seemed to sense what she was thinking because he straightened and moved ominously toward her.

Her scathing words tumbled out. "You talked about phoning my husband at the cottage. If you'd been inside the place, you'd know there wasn't a phone. And when I was down there this afternoon there weren't any new car tracks. You may have seen my husband since he went to Los Angeles, but it wasn't at the——"

"He was in L.A.?" Anger roughened his words.

Surprise caught her unawares. "Why yes! You mean you didn't know?"

"I mean I'm through talking." The indolence was gone now as he approached. "If you haven't got the money on you—I reckon you left it in the car." He looked triumphant at her sudden chagrin. "Let's have the keys."

"You have no right. . . ."

"I said let's have the keys." He was close beside her. "I wouldn't mind searching." Strong fingers squeezed her wrist suggestively.

"Keep your hands off me!" She struggled to pull her

147

hand away and yanked her key ring from her pocket. "Take the money. It's in a bag in the trunk. I was a fool not to have gone to the police in the first place."

He caught the keys neatly without letting her go. "There wasn't much risk. I knew you'd want to keep your husband's reputation intact. Now, I have to find a place to put you for a while."

"You mean you're not going to let me get help for Ernie?"

"And have you blabbing everything to the State Police before I can get beyond the city limits? Not a chance, sister. I'm not sure though, exactly how long to keep you." He eyed her suggestively. "Of course the steam room up by the peeler would take care of my problem permanently."

Jean remembered the room at the end of the building where logs were dumped to soften them for peeling. A human being wouldn't last long in the soaring temperatures. "Why take that risk?" she got out finally. "A murder charge wouldn't help your record."

"Who's talking about murder? If somebody's fool enough to stumble in the steam room...."

"Nobody stumbles in that steam room. Even the newest member of the bull gang knows that. Certainly the guards do." She kept her voice level with an effort. "You wouldn't have time to spend even half your money before they caught up with you."

He hesitated. "All right—I'll skip that idea because I've just thought of a better one. We'll go up to the mill." He yanked at her arm and brought her close to his side. "There's always the saw room. Once I truss you up in there, you'll be out of circulation until the day shift. With your hands tied behind your back and a rope around your ankles, you'll be hogtied for sure. C'mon, stop dragging your feet." He twisted her wrist to enforce his demand, obviously enjoying her involuntary cry of pain.

"But what about Ernie?" she said desperately.

"What about him? Indians have thick skulls. When he wakes up with a headache, he'll learn to keep his eyes open next time he starts trailing somebody."

148

"It wouldn't hurt to call a doctor," she protested, taking a last look over her shoulder.

"Give up. Be thankful you're getting out of this with your head in one piece."

Jean nodded mutely in response to his jibe. She was unable to speak after the shock of looking back and discovering that Ernie's fallen body had disappeared. If the bartender had been feigning unconsciousness, then he must have heard the entire discussion. In his groggy state, he probably decided it would be better to help her later rather than risking a fight right then.

"You're sure quiet, lady."

She almost stammered in her confusion. "I'm sorry . . . I was thinking. . . ."

"Don't bother with any bright ideas—they won't work. I'm gonna plant you smack in the middle of a pile of those circular saws. With the ten-inch teeth on those babies, you're apt to cut right through an arm or a leg if you tried to sever the ropes."

She shuddered. "You don't have to keep on. I get the picture."

"I wanted you to be sure. 'Course if you want to bleed to death up there in the mill, go right ahead." He pulled her to a stop and put his shoulder against a big sliding door. "Stay there. I want to close this so the watchman won't get suspicious."

For the moment he turned his back and in that instant Jean felt a strong hand grasp her shoulder and yank her sharply to one side.

Another figure brushed by her and swung her captor roughly around, taking advantage of the other's confusion to explode a powerful jab to his ribs and, as he folded over in pain, a lethal uppercut to the jaw. It was done so coldly, so decisively, that the man collapsed without a sound other than his first surprised gurgle.

"My god, Grant," Toby criticized from Jean's side. "You didn't have to be so rough on him."

"The hell he didn't," Ernie said, emerging from the shadow. "I'd like to use something harder than a fist on

149

him." He was rubbing the back of his head gingerly. "I still can't see straight."

Grant kneaded the knuckles of his right hand. "I told you to wait in the car, Ernie."

"Not a chance. I wouldn't have missed that." He stared at the fallen figure impassively.

"Well, fun's over," Toby said. "No scalping tonight, Chief. I'll take you and our heroine over to the car."

Jean was standing in a trance, still hearing the sickening explosion of bone against flesh in that brief, furious onslaught. She swayed slightly.

Grant materialized instantly at her side. "Are you all right?" It was hard to tell from that level tone what his feeling was . . . or if there was any feeling at all.

She nodded.

"Can you drive Ernie to a doctor?"

"Of course." She took a deep breath and the world resumed its proper shape. "What about you and Toby?"

"We'll wait here for the State Patrol. They shouldn't be long. We called them after Doreen found your note." He slanted a dispassionate look at her. "Is it any use asking why you walked into this like a half-witted idiot?"

She cast about for an answer and finally summoned her pride to cloak the truth. Certainly she couldn't admit she had acted like a half-witted idiot to preserve her husband's future. Especially when that same husband was treating her like an interloper on sacred ground.

"Well?" he repeated.

"Sorry," she said flippantly. "The witness refuses to answer."

"Stop it, you two," Toby protested. "Didn't you hear the bell? The fight's over."

"Forget it, Toby." Jean's light tone was a triumph. "Poor Ernie's waiting for help and I'm driving the ambulance." She turned slightly. "Do I say thank you, Grant?"

"It isn't necessary."

"All right then—I'll just say good night." She paused and ventured once more. "Will I see you at the house later tonight?"

"No." There was no indecision in his answer although there were lines of strain around his eyes. "I expect to be here until late and I'll go straight on to the cottage."

"Fine!" she lied.

"Good night, Jean."

Probably, she decided, he couldn't wait to get her out from underfoot. She kept her back ramrod-straight all the way to the car. Some people would have called it a strategic retreat.

The more honest souls would have acknowledged it was a total defeat.

Chapter TEN

When Toby appeared at the house the following noon, Doreen met him at the front door and greeted him in the traditionally approved manner of engaged couples.

Finally she pulled herself out of his embrace, smoothed her hair complacently, and said, "I suppose you're expecting lunch. . . ."

"Now there's enthusiasm for you. Of course, I'm expecting lunch. Haven't you heard . . . engagements are a testing time. This is when I learn whether you're *cordon bleu* or whether I'll have to exist on TV dinners."

"What if the result comes out TV dinners?"

"Then I can take cooking lessons or look around for a blonde who specializes in paella Valenciana."

"You could also go on a diet," she said severely. "Most American men eat too much."

He whacked his middle with the flat of his hand. "Strong as a rock . . . not an extra ounce of flesh." Suddenly he sniffed the delectable odor wafting its way from the kitchen. "That doesn't smell like a frozen dinner."

"I should hope not. It's beef Stroganoff." She cut

him down to size quickly. "Mrs. Lloyd believes people need a hearty lunch."

"I could always propose to Mrs. Lloyd."

"You could try," she said fairly. "Of course Mr. Lloyd poses a slight problem. It might be more practical if we tried to hire her to cook for us."

"That's my girl." Toby patted her head approvingly. "Thinking, always thinking. Unfortunately, Jean and Grant would come after her and us with a shotgun."

"I don't think Jean will need her in New Orleans." Doreen nodded toward the hall phone. "She's calling the airport right now to confirm space on the evening plane."

"Oh no!"

"Oh yes! Come on, let's go out to the patio. You can be deciding on ways to change her mind over lunch. At least, I hope you can. I've been arguing all morning and I haven't made a dent."

"Damn!" Toby said softly. "Talk about a pair of stubborn idiots. . . ."

"Watch it, friend." Jean came up behind him at the sliding patio door. "Those are fighting words in this part of the world."

He rounded on her with exasperation, noting her pale face and the pink swollen eyelids which weren't camouflaged by a hasty application of powder. "Now look, Jean . . ." he began.

"No, you look," she interrupted. "If you're just having lunch—that's fine. If you're giving a pep talk for men in general or even one in particular—the door's right over there."

"But you haven't given Grant a chance. . . ."

She went over to a side serving table and surveyed the bottles on it. "That's a matter of opinion. In the meantime, you're not John Alden and my name isn't Priscilla—so the similarity stops. Do you want some sherry?"

"I could do with something stronger," he growled.

"Then help yourself to the bar in the living room," she instructed calmly. "Doreen?"

"Sherry's fine for me." That young lady stretched

back in a rattan chair like a lazy cat. "If you two don't stop arguing, you'll ruin your digestion."

Toby shrugged. "All right. For the sake of beef Stroganoff, I'll be a perfect gentleman. I'll even drink sherry."

"That's mighty big of you," Jean told him filling a glass and handing it over. "Since you're one of my favorite people, I'll forgive you this time." She stood on tiptoe and bestowed a light kiss on his cheek.

"Keep that up and I'll put you on that plane to New Orleans myself," Doreen warned. "I suppose you confirmed your space?"

"Uh-huh." Deftly Jean changed the subject. "Now . . . what's new on your wedding plans. Did you decide to build on the ocean lot?"

That safe subject kept all three of them engrossed during the main course and through a delectable chocolate soufflé, which had Toby groaning after a mammoth second helping. It wasn't until they were relaxing over cups of coffee that Jean herself referred to the night before.

"If Grant's trip to Los Angeles had anything to do with the future of the plywood plant, I suppose I'd better hear about it," she said abruptly. "I've been expecting Bart to call to discuss that Midwestern offer."

Toby stirred uneasily in his chair and avoided looking at Doreen. "I doubt that Bart will be calling for a while, Jean. After the news Grant unearthed . . ."

Doreen interrupted him. "Stop being tactful, Toby. Jean might as well learn the truth now. Uncle Bart didn't call because he's in this mess right up to his neck." She was staring at her coffee spoon as if she'd never seen one before. "I wouldn't blame you if you threw me out in the road, but honestly I didn't know anything about it."

Jean leaned over to squeeze her hand reassuringly. "I'm sure you didn't, so stop fretting. Frankly, I'm utterly confused. Could you start from the beginning?"

"All right," Toby said. "The beginning was when Grant and I took a look at the plant's books. Grant

154

couldn't figure out why the sales were so low when the product potential was so great." He reached for a cigarette and then, with an apologetic grimace, belatedly offered one to Doreen. Once they were lit, he went on. "Grant told me he mentioned the type of research stressed in his lab."

Jean nodded.

"Well, it seemed to him that there could be a direct tie-in with their research results if his company would approve. He thought it was worth a trip to Los Angeles to find out. However, after the brake trouble, he didn't want to leave you here alone, so he persuaded Ernie to leave his bartending for a few days and play watchdog over you."

"You mean Ernie has been following me around for days?"

"It wasn't much of a job," he replied mildly. "You stayed in the house most of the time. It was only when you made that last-minute trip to the bank that Ernie became suspicious." He grinned at her discomfort. "He wasn't the only one. My secretary was sure you were up to something when she saw you receive all that folding money."

"There's nothing sacred around here," Jean murmured.

"It's a darned good thing for you there isn't! Ernie provided a delaying action if nothing else."

"I realize that," she said with some compunction. "Actually I checked with his wife this morning and she told me he's feeling pretty well—all things considered." A wrinkle creased her forehead. "She mentioned something about their looking forward to his new job."

"He's going to start as a sales trainee at the plant. Grant thinks he'll be terrific," Toby said. "Now Mrs. Ravenwing can give up all those side jobs."

"It sounds great. What does Bart say?"

"Bart is giving up his interest." Toby tapped the ash from his cigarette. "He's decided the plywood company no longer needs him."

"It wasn't voluntary," Doreen put in grimly. "After

155

Grant and Toby finished talking to him last night, he would have agreed to anything if they'd promise not to prosecute."

Seeing Jean's bewildered expression, Toby took up the story. "It's this way, honey. Bart was the one who originally hired George Smith."

"You mean the man at the plant who hit Ernie?"

"The one and only. I forgot you weren't introduced. That's his honest-to-God name even if it does sound phony."

"We skipped the social amenities," Jean said dryly.

"Just as well—he's pretty unsavory. When it was apparent that Grant was trying to find out about Smith, Bart decided his connection with him could be dangerous, so he told Smith to get out."

"You mean he paid him off," Doreen put in.

"Probably—but there's no way to prove it. I suspect that Foster was encouraged to leave as well. Those production figures were kept low only with management approval—a poor balance sheet made the Midwest offer look more attractive. Foster was probably well paid for his part in it and decided to leave when we started asking embarrassing questions." He drew in on his cigarette thoughtfully. "Smith will find it considerably harder to leave town. At the moment, he's in custody and charged with attempted extortion, assault, and is under suspicion for that Los Angeles lab explosion. If he talks, and the authorities think he will— Bart could be in serious trouble."

"I don't think they'll be able to prove he was behind it," Jean said slowly.

"Maybe not," Toby agreed, "but the circumstances will ruin his position as a reputable businessman. When we finished talking to him last night, he'd aged about ten years. Frankly, I think he'll give up on all his interests."

"He does have trouble with his heart," Doreen added. "He had a legitimate doctor's appointment that afternoon you were in the car accident. If he had instructed Smith to damage those brakes, it's a

156

wonder he didn't have a serious attack from the excitement."

"Bart isn't admitting anything," Toby said, "but I'll bet he okayed the car scheme thinking it was another kind of harassment like the fire outbreak at the plant. Of course, if Grant had been put out of commission for a while it would have helped his cause. I don't think he meant to injure you, Jean."

Her lips tightened. "I'd rather not think about it."

"That's probably the best way," he said gently, leaning forward to extinguish his cigarette. "How about pouring me some more coffee?"

"Of course." She picked up the ceramic pot. "Doreen?"

"No thanks. There's been so much excitement that I should be drinking hot milk."

"I know." Jean put the coffeepot back down on the warming tray and got up to prowl restlessly around the patio. "There was no need for the doctor to treat me last night as well as Ernie."

"Grant called him after you left the plant," Toby said. "He was afraid that you wouldn't get any rest otherwise."

"I see." Her lips tightened. It was just as if Grant were sitting on the patio with them. She wondered bleakly if his ghost would be beside her on the plane to New Orleans as well. Down deep, there was the niggling suspicion that he would haunt her for the rest of her life, no matter how hard she tried to forget him.

"Maybe feminine curiosity is overrated," Toby was complaining.

Her head bobbed up. "I beg your pardon?"

"Don't you want to know why Smith put the finger on you? You might appear a little anxious."

"Of course I want to know."

"You don't look anxious," he continued, giving her a cryptic glance. "You look as if you didn't give a damn about anything at the moment."

"Stop browbeating her, Toby," Doreen commanded. "She has other things on her mind."

Jean gave her a grateful smile. "Why *did* Smith pick on me?"

Toby took a sip of coffee before replying. "The way I figure it, he wanted more money. There was only one person to logically supply it."

"Grant might have been interested. . . ."

He shook his head. "You're out of your mind. Grant knew that he didn't have anything to worry about, so why should he pay Smith to keep quiet? Nope . . ." He leaned back in his chair. "You were the obvious patsy."

"Thanks very much."

"Well, you were," he insisted. "All he had to do was wait until Grant was out of the way and then make sure you received his note."

"How could he know that I wouldn't get in touch with Grant?"

"Because Bart had told him that both Grant and I wanted a conference as soon as Grant got off the plane. Since your husband was already a day later than he planned in getting back, he knew there wouldn't be any time lost in getting together. Smith figured it would be safe to contact you in the interval. As soon as he saw you get the money from the bank, he knew he'd won the gamble. Of course, he didn't know that Grant had been in Los Angeles checking on him after ferreting out his name from the plywood company records. And he didn't know that Ernie was going to be dogging your footsteps when you went for the payoff."

"I'd like to have known it myself," Jean told him. "It would have helped my morale considerably."

"Don't kid me. If you had heard it was Grant's idea, you would have gone through the roof."

Doreen cut in with diplomatic haste. "It was fortunate that Toby's secretary called when she did."

He nodded and explained to Jean. "We were just about finished talking with Bart—for the first time last night—when she finally called me. She had been stewing about your collecting all that money at the bank. We knew something was wrong and when we stopped by the house, we found your note saying that you had gone to the plant. Grant didn't even want to waste time calling State Police headquarters before going after you."

"I've never seen him look so wild," Doreen confirmed.

Jean perched on the edge of a raised brick flower bed and made a helpless gesture. "I'm sorry I alarmed all of you. When I read Smith's note, I didn't stop to think rationally."

"Well, you weren't alone in that," Toby assured her. "Grant and I were practically flying low by the time we got out to the plant. It's a good thing we didn't meet much traffic. Fortunately, Ernie came stumbling out the side door just as we arrived and was able to fill us in. Then, all we had to do was intercept Smith and you know the rest."

She nodded.

Doreen cupped her chin in her palm and said thoughtfully, "I heard that Grant went after Smith like somebody possessed. Of course, he probably remembered that California explosion and wanted revenge. That could be one explanation." She eyed Jean curiously. "I didn't know he was so primitive."

Toby was amused at her innocence. "The veneer of civilization runs exceedingly thin in most of us. Remember that, woman, if you're tempted to get out of line."

"Why? Is your right uppercut as good as Grant's?"

"I doubt it." He flexed his fist. "But with luck I could manage ten rounds with you."

"Very funny." She flushed as Jean stifled a laugh. "It's a good thing I took those karate lessons."

"Stop it, you two," Jean commanded mildly. "You can fight when you're alone." She turned to Toby. "What's going to happen now?"

"That's up to you, isn't it?" He gave her a level look. "As far as the plant goes, things couldn't be better. Thanks to Grant, we'll have a new product to sell and customers waiting to buy it." He hunched forward in his chair. "Down in California, Grant and his lab staff were working on an improved resin for plywood shipping containers. Just before the explosion, they succeeded in developing a composite panel far

159

superior to anything on the market. The shippers are enthusiastic because the new resin-glass composite will save them millions of dollars in the long run." He grinned. "I'm enthusiastic because Grant's company has agreed to let us use the process on a percentage basis."

"What about Bart's voting stock?"

"Grant suggested he sell it to the employees so they can share in the future profits. They can elect their own member to the board of directors afterwards."

"Is Bart going to do it?"

"Of course he is." Toby was emphatic. "If he has a chance of selling some stock to stay out of jail, he won't even hesitate. He even makes a profit this way, but not the nice bundle he planned."

Jean bent over to weed under a marigold plant. "No wonder he wanted us to sell out."

He shrugged and leaned back in his chair. "There probably was a similar process nearing completion at a laboratory in the Midwest. It could have been behind his job offer to Grant too. When that failed, there was the convenient explosion in the lab to delay things." He shook his head. "Bart's a mighty determined fellow when it comes to getting what he wants."

"He always has been," Doreen concurred. "It was too bad he didn't come up against someone like Grant before."

Toby nodded agreement. "Just like two slabs of granite meeting head-on. Something had to give."

There was a short silence. Then Jean asked, "Is Grant going to stay and run the plant?" From the casual interest she displayed, she might have been inquiring about a grocery ad.

"So you finally got around to it!" Toby said sharply. "I know you're above such things at the moment, but a lot of people's paychecks depend on that very point."

"Watch it, Toby," Doreen warned.

He flashed her an apologetic glance before turning back to Jean and speaking very distinctly. "Grant hasn't the slightest intention of running the mill. He pointed out to Bart and me that he was merely supervising your interests when he poked his nose in all this. He went on to say that he likes his job in California and he intends to return as soon as his leave is over."

"So?" Her wooden monosyllable gave nothing away. Not her despair nor the collapse of her hopes after his terse pronouncement.

"So don't be a damned fool, woman! Just because Grant's as stubborn as you are—don't play the farce indefinitely." Toby shoved back his chair and stood up. "The plant needs him, this whole town needs him and boy! . . . do *you* need him! You've been wandering around like Madame Butterfly waiting for Lieutenant Pinkerton ever since he rented my cottage."

"All right," Jean answered in a low tone to hide the raw pain in her voice. "Suppose you're right. Suppose I do wish he'd stay." Her hands were clenched tightly at her sides. "He won't call me . . . or talk to me . . . or come near this house. What am I to do, Toby? Crawl to him?"

"Jeanie . . . Jeanie," he chided, strolling over and putting a comforting arm around her shoulders. "I thought you had more sense. Of course you don't crawl. You walk—straight north along the beach about a mile."

She stared at him. "You mean that I should go to the cottage?"

"Now you're getting the idea." He gave her a quick hug and then moved over to the patio steps. "From what I hear, an apology's in order and you'd better deliver it personally. I don't think Grant will be un-reasonable."

"But Toby, how can I be sure?"

He went on as if she hadn't spoken. "Low tide comes about six o'clock. Should be a good night for agate hunting too." He glanced at his watch. "Now I'm late for an appointment at the golf club with a man who wants to buy some real estate. Doreen, you can carry my golf bag and watch me close the deal."

"You're so kind," Doreen murmured sarcastically, but she got up promptly all the same. "What do I get out of this?"

161

"A free golf lesson . . . and afterwards a cup of coffee if you don't talk when I'm putting. Thanks for the lunch, Jeanie. Remember what I said about that walk. . . ." He shot her a humorous look. "Keep your head down if you hunt for agates on the beach. . . ."

"Why?"

"Then when you meet him you'll give the proper impression—subdued and in the presence of the master."

"Toby, you fool!" Doreen hurriedly grasped his arm. "Pay no attention to him, Jean. We're going now." She pushed him toward the car and hesitated just long enough to add, "But he's right, you know," before she grinned impishly and hurried after him.

Her words stayed in Jean's mind all afternoon as she aimlessly wandered around the house. Two suitcases were open on her bed, but she hesitated over packing them. If she did walk to the cottage and apologize to Grant, perhaps she wouldn't have to go away. But if she apologized and he still acted the way he had last night, then there was no alternative.

She frowned and moved purposefully toward her bedroom. She could pack one bag and ask Doreen to send the rest of her things later. There was no point, she sternly told herself, in wondering what might happen if Grant's mood softened. It was impossible to tell whether their hasty marriage ceremony had been anything to him other than sheer necessity. Of course he had kissed her once. . . . She sank down on the edge of the bed and put her fingers to her lips as she remembered. How could one kiss leave such a searing memory! Resolutely she shook her head and stood up. A kiss didn't mean a thing.

She moved over to her dressing table and pulled open the top drawer. At least she could brush her hair and decide what to wear if she did walk down to the cottage. It should be something casual, she decided, because everybody knew you didn't hunt agates dressed for high tea. On the other hand, if Grant invited her to have a cup of tea, it would be nice to be wearing something flattering.

She made a face in the mirror as her brush caught in a snarl of hair. Then she took another incredulous look before snatching the tiny whisk broom from her hair and slamming it back in the drawer. Good heavens, if she kept on this way she'd need a guide to find her way up the beach!

When it was finally time to leave, she exhibited all the poise of a thirteen-year-old on her first date. Her palms felt like the inside of an oyster and she jumped with surprise when the clock struck six.

Doreen and Toby had stayed pointedly away for the afternoon, so there ere no curious glances as she stole to the front door. There was muted noise in the kitchen, where Mrs. Lloyd was starting dinner but Jean saw no reason to explain her walk at sunset. If she tarried, Mrs. Lloyd would observe her beige slacks with the tiny butterscotch plaid which fitted so trimly around the hips. There would be comments because the slacks were obviously brand new. So was the matching cashmere tunic which clung discreetly at specific intervals. There was also a fingertip-length beige nylon windbreaker to be whisked off in case she *was* invited to tea.

Before leaving the shelter of the porch, she tied an emerald silk scarf under her chin to preserve her hair style. There was no reason to repeat that other venture when she arrived tousled and dripping.

The grass path down to the stairs was deserted although she could see the bright color of Rick's bike on the road beyond. A fleeting smile touched her lips as she thought of the youngster. If he could call at the cottage to inquire after Homer's health, so could she. Such a patently flimsy excuse might soften Grant's mood so that her apology about the bikini would be better received.

She paused at the top of the steep wooden steps at the cliff edge and surveyed the expanse of beach below. There were a few energetic children playing "Keepaway" from the waves, but otherwise the solitude was pleasantly inviting. Perhaps, she decided, there was something to be said for the corporation's beach rules after all.

The customary south wind pushed gently at her back when she turned north at the foot of the steps. She carefully negotiated the tumbled driftwood at the high tide mark and made her way down to the firm, damp sand. Since she was trying to make a good impression, she would keep her canvas sneakers dry as long as possible. She stopped to brush a piece of seaweed from her shoelace, so she was unprepared for the masculine hail behind her.

"Hey Jean—wait a minute!"

She turned, shading her eyes. "Ernie! What are you doing here? You're supposed to be resting."

"Who wants to rest any more? I feel fine." His ruddy face creased with laughter as he gestured up toward the driftwood. "I was sitting up there on a log deciding that I'm a very lucky fellow—thanks to your husband."

She beamed in return. "I heard about your new job. It sounds wonderful. We're all delighted that you'll be at the plant."

"I'm looking forward to the sales angle. It'll be a change from my job at the Inn." He rubbed the side of his nose reflectively.

"You mean, after you've seen one martini you've seen them all."

"Just about."

"Well, if you get lonesome, you can always go back and sit on the other side of the bar."

"Not me," he said emphatically. "I have other ways to spend my money." He glanced at the tide mark beside them. "Time to be getting home. We're going out tonight for a little celebration." Intercepting her anxious look, he added hastily, "It's o.k. The doc knows it's going to be a very quiet celebration with no bouncing around."

"I should hope so," she chided.

"Don't worry. I don't want anything to go wrong now."

She put out a hand to stop him as he turned. "Ernie

—thanks for watching over me these past days. It was kind of you to help."

He shrugged wide shoulders. "Forget it. I'm glad there's no need to worry any longer. . . . That husband of yours knows what he's doing." He frowned briefly. "You're late. The tide's turned already. You'd better get moving if you're going around the Rock without a soaking."

"Darn! I thought I had plenty of time. Toby must have looked at the wrong tide table."

He chuckled. "Mr. Calhoun has his mind on too many things these days to be thinking straight."

She nodded as she knotted the scarf more firmly under her chin. "One thing, I think . . . and she's very pretty."

"That's for sure. It's too bad we're limited to brunettes. I always thought a redhead in the tribe would add a little excitement."

"Any more of that talk and I'll tell the doctor you have a delayed concussion."

He tapped his forehead carefully. "Almost as good as new. Get going or you won't make it around the point. Give my regards to your husband."

"I will. See you." She waved briefly and turned to continue up the beach at a fast walk.

The closer she got to Wailing Rock, the more evident it became that Ernie's tidal reckoning was far more accurate than Toby's. Already some of the billowy combers were saturating the rocks with spray.

She started up the rock terrace paying scant heed to the colorful tidal pools, but carefully watching where she placed her feet. This was not the time to take a header on the barnacles and end up with scraped knees under torn slacks!

She smiled slightly, anticipating her arrival at the cottage. This time, she'd be cool and reasonable as she presented her apology. If Grant asked her in for a frank discussion of their marital affairs, she'd show him that she could excel in that department too!

Her foot slipped slightly on an uneven rock face forcing her abruptly out of her dream world. It would be best to get around the point before making any more plans. She bent over and went up the next-to-the-last rock on all fours, pausing at the top to survey that narrow crevice on the end. As she watched, a wave splashed again, showering the aperture in fine mist. Evidently the tide had advanced considerably. There was no hope for it but to duck down and watch her chance on the incoming breakers. If she timed it right, she could manage without getting damp.

She waited impatiently for a few minutes, trying to gauge the height of each incoming roller. Finally she made a grimace of disgust. At that rate, she'd be stuck for the rest of the night. It was better to—what was it the British said—"Have a go at it."

"All right," she murmured uneasily, "I'll have a go at it—right now."

Still crouching, she slithered down the other side of the rock and hurried to the point. She spread-eagled the vertical rock face carefully and, inhaling, edged around. So far, so good, she thought exultantly, although moving nose to nose on a damp slab of rock had its disadvantages. She'd have to hurry or one of the strong breakers would arrive. Wasn't there a belief about the seventh wave being the biggest?

Frantically she edged through the narrow space and backed down the other side, her foot searching for the toehold to break that five-foot drop to the beach. Searching . . . searching . . . and finding! She'd done it! Her muscles tensed for the final drop and she released her hold just as the next wave hit the bottom of the rock.

There was a confused instant in the icy spray before she hit the beach. Then came the chilling reality of salt water surging around her knees.

"Oh no!" she wailed.

The wave receded and she was left standing there— a soaking, miserable figure so woebegone that, for the moment, she wished she could just float out with the undertow. Finally she reached down and wrung out a dripping corner of her coat. The soaked slacks clung to her legs like an adhesive label.

"Damn!" she said forcefully. "Damn, damn, DAMN!"

"Don't lose your temper now," Grant said from a few feet away. "Have you ever thought of carrying a parachute?" He waded toward her, comfortably clad in shorts and a sweat shirt.

"Very funny." Dismally she turned toward him. "It's all right for you to talk . . . *your* clothes haven't been ruined." She made a stricken gesture downward. "I'm a mess. And I wanted to look nice." As she heard those infantile words tremble out, it became evident that her plan for a cool, sophisticated approach had also taken a header in the water.

He took her arm. "If we get up on shore, you might still be able to salvage some of that outfit."

"I can't . . ." she let herself be led, "I look just as bad as last time." Her glance flicked over him accusingly. "You didn't even get wet."

"Is that bad? I just dressed for the occasion."

"What occasion?" she wanted to know.

"Hunting agates, of course." He plunged his hand into his pocket and pulled out some multicolored specimens. "Nothing spectacular, but there's one that shows promise. It's too bad you've left it so late—now that the tide's turned the good agate bed is under water."

She snatched her arm away. "What about surf fishing then?" she asked furiously. "I can't get much wetter."

"And have you get chilled? Don't be silly. You should be in bed after that ducking." The same arm was taken in a firmer grip. "If you keep on with these escapades, you'd better hire the doctor on a monthly retainer fee."

Her feet dragged as they approached the cottage. To be invited when she was in command of the situation was one thing; being towed in like an unwelcome bur was another.

"There's no need for all this bother," she said. "If you'll get me a newspaper, I won't drip too much on your car's upholstery. I can change when I get home."

"It's no bother," he assured her carelessly, "but I'm afraid you're stuck with my hospitality for the moment."

This time she pulled to a complete stop.

"No car?" Her tone was ominous.

"No car." He made a helpless gesture. "Of course if I'd known, I wouldn't have lent it to Doreen."

"What's the matter with Doreen's car?"

"I've no idea." He slid open the long window and stepped politely aside. "Should I have asked?"

"Yes . . . er . . . I don't know." She hesitated and then, feeling extremely foolish, walked stiffly past him into the cottage. "It did seem like an unusual coincidence."

He merely raised his eyebrows.

She felt the blood rush to her cheeks at his unspoken rebuke. "I'm dripping on your rug," she said finally. "If I could change. . . ."

Silently he walked down the hall and opened the bathroom door. "There are clean towels on the hamper. A hot shower might be a good idea."

The door was closed firmly behind her before she could reply.

She stood in the middle of the room and then risked a glance in the mirror of the medicine cabinet. Darn! Just as bad as she feared. Her head scarf had slithered onto her shoulders and currently resembled a soggy green noose. As for her hair itself—sadly she shook her head and moved to turn on the shower faucets. The only solution was to shampoo out the salt water.

The hot shower helped both her chilled condition and her morale. By the time she had dried herself on one of the thick orange towels, she felt like life had its acceptable moments. Carefully she wrapped the towel around her, sarong-fashion, and piled her wet clothing neatly on the side of the tub. She stood erect, thinking that Grant was taking a long time to find something for her to wear. Unfortunately she couldn't wander out in his living room clad only in a bath towel to complain about the service. Nor did she relish putting her tousled head around the door and calling for a pair of corduroy trousers. It was a pity that Doreen had collected her bikini outfit. Not—she told herself hastily— that she would have chosen to wear it, but it did have

168

several notable advantages over wool socks and a pair of man's pants.

Her gaze fastened thoughtfully on Grant's green silk bathrobe, which was again hanging on the back of the door. It had certainly covered her adequately before. There was a moment of indecision, then she slipped it off the hook and draped her towel over the hamper.

The oversized robe was as discreet as she remembered. Humming cheerfully, she tied the belt and went over to filch Grant's comb from the medicine cabinet. When she was finished with it, she rinsed it carefully and put it back on the shelf. That done, she made a final survey in the mirror. Green silk had its advantages, after all. The vital thing to remember about the robe was to keep the belt tight. Otherwise the deep collar parted in unexpected Mod fashion.

She padded hesitantly out into the hall. Hearing Grant still moving around in the balcony bedroom, she gathered confidence and decided the kitchen was her next logical stop. An ocean ducking at least warranted a cup of coffee.

Once she had put the water on to boil, gnawing hunger pangs encouraged her to reconnoiter further. With luck there might be something in the refrigerator besides bacon and eggs.

There was. Jean's eyes widened at the festive array. Cold roast chicken, molded aspic salad with shrimp, a plateful of French pastries bursting with calories, and three bottles of champagne. She pulled a bottle out carefully and raised her eyebrows at the impressive vintage on the label. When Grant entertained, he did it with a vengeance!

She replaced the wine and let the refrigerator door click softly closed. From the looks of the food, Grant was planning for company later in the evening. Her unhappy gaze fell on a plate of cocktail crackers nearby and she reached over for one to nibble. It would be nice to be on his guest list, at least. Strange that Doreen and Toby hadn't said anything about a party. She took another cracker and wandered out in the living room while she waited for the coffee water to boil.

Storm clouds on the horizon had subdued the sunset colors and the freshening wind was catching pieces of spindrift from the crest of the breakers and whirling them into the sea. The gray Pacific looked threatening and she felt suddenly grateful for the warmth and security of the cottage. It was certainly not the night to be out on the water.

She hugged the dressing gown to her as she turned toward the pickle jar in the corner. "Be thankful you have your own little pond, Homer. You wouldn't last a minute out there tonight. . . ." Her voice trailed off as she became aware of the latest model in aquariums standing in solitary grandeur on the table top. The inside furnishings of the tank were so lavish that it took a moment for Jean to find Homer's slender shape among the grasses and filter pump.

She went down on her knees and stared at the transformed goldfish. Homer was swimming briskly and purposefully among the floating weeds. By his side swam a gorgeous gold fantail. Each flip of her fins was seductive artistry in motion. No wonder Homer was blowing bubbles!

Jean sank back respectfully. "Homer—you've hit the jackpot."

"I take it you approve." Grant was coming down the balcony steps after changing into flannel slacks and a velour sports shirt.

Jean got to her feet and adjusted the robe carefully. "Of course," she said, trying to indicate that she was equally at ease in a bathrobe or a ball gown. "For a man who doesn't like goldfish, you've a strange way of showing it."

"The poor little cuss looked lonely swimming around in that jar. I could imagine how he felt."

Her hands fluttered to check the tightness of her belt. "Well, he certainly won't be lonely now. He'll probably have a stroke swimming all those extra laps. What's the name of his new chum—Jethroe?"

"You have no imagination." Grant went over to pull the drapes over the front windows and then knelt to drop a match onto the fireplace kindling. "Does that look like a Jethroe to you? Rick calls her Cleo. He swears her ancestors came straight from the Nile."

She smiled ruefully. "I don't know about that, but it's obvious Homer isn't missing his pickle jar one little bit." She moved over and warmed her hands at the crackling fire. After an uneasy interval, she couldn't stand it any longer. She took a deep breath and asked, "Do I make my apologies now or wait until after we've had coffee?"

He lounged against the arm of the davenport. "That all depends. How badly is your conscience bothering you?"

"Stop fencing with me." She rounded on him fiercely. "It's hard enough to get through this."

"Then stop making such a project out of it. Come over here and sit down." He indicated the cushion beside him. "You look as if you're ready to bolt out the door. Do I frighten you so much?"

She didn't answer but approached warily until she dared meet the warmth of that familiar gray glance, watched his firm lips take a tender upwards quirk, and felt her heart thud in response. How could she ever have been afraid of this man?

"Grant, I'm sorry I was such an idiot." The words tumbled out. "Doreen told me about the bikini and Toby reported what a wonderful job you've done about the mess at the plant. Even Ernie sent his best when I met him on the beach. Everyone wants you to stay and work here." She sank down beside him and absently pulled the robe tighter. "You needn't feel any further obligation to me if you do stay."

"How did you work that out?"

"The ceremony can be annulled. After all, we didn't . . . we haven't . . ." She hesitated until it became obvious he wasn't going to help her out. She floundered on, "The way things are, I mean. You can start legal proceedings here or I can do it in New Orleans. I have a plane reservation at midnight."

"You *had* a plane reservation," he corrected calmly. "I canceled it."

Jean felt as if her lungs were going to burst. "I don't believe it," she said finally.

He pulled her hands into his lap. "Better get used to believing it, idiot. I've decided to hang onto my addle-pated wife."

"But Grant . . ."

"No. You pay attention to me for a minute." Gently, he pushed back a strand of her hair which had fallen over her temple. "Of course I canceled that reservation just as soon as Toby and Doreen told me about it. I've been keeping my fingers crossed that you'd come to see me all afternoon. If you hadn't, I was all set to drive to the airport and take you off the plane by brute force."

"Your car is gone. . . ."

"My car is just up around the bend in the road."

"Then you could have taken me home," she breathed, still unable to fully comprehend the utter joy flooding over her.

His eyes darkened. "I thought you *had* come home. Haven't you, darling?"

"Oh yes, Grant . . . please." Her words were soft, almost incoherent. "I'd like that very much."

"There's something I'd like more," he muttered, scooping her in a close embrace, "and I don't intend to wait any longer."

That possessive kiss went on and on. Finally Jean pushed back just far enough to catch her breath.

"Sorry, darling," Grant said, resting his chin on her soft hair. "I didn't mean to overwhelm you. What a time I've had keeping away from you all these days."

She turned her head slightly and let her lips rest against his tanned throat. "You certainly didn't give any hints in that direction. I thought you couldn't stand the sight of me."

He looked down at her in fond exasperation. "Well, I didn't get much cooperation from you. Lounges in the bedroom! If you hadn't been frozen with fright that night, I would have kissed you then." He pulled her across his lap and she buried her nose in his shoulder.

"I wish you had," she confessed. "You wouldn't have met much resistance." She raised her head. "Why did

172

you insist on that marriage ceremony, Grant? Really and truly, I mean."

"For the reasons I told you about."

"I see."

He shook her gently. "No, you don't. There were a few more reasons besides. I'm sorry the wedding was so cut and dried. . . . We'll make up for it on our honeymoon." His hand tilted up her chin. "Let me look at you."

She made a shy gesture. "I'm such a ravishing figure at the moment."

His eyes moved with amusement over the silk dressing gown. She tried to tuck her bare feet under the hem and unwittingly pulled it tighter, giving it a far different effect from the modest one for which she was striving.

"You'll do." The uneven timbre of his voice belied the laconic words. "I decided to keep you around when I pulled you out of the water the first time."

"You said you didn't want to be tied down."

"Pay attention to what a man does—not what he says. If you'll remember, the first thing I did was get your name on a marriage license."

"It was my devastating first impression," she said, smiling. "Seaweed threaded through my hair and sand on my chin."

"Well, you hit a responsive chord. I'm partial to women wearing clinging slacks."

She flushed. "At least that time you were a gentleman and offered me some clothes."

"I'm still a gentleman." He grinned slowly. "But there is a difference."

"Oh?"

"We weren't married then." This time there was no mistaking the devilment in his eyes.

The warmth spreading through Jean's body had nothing to do with the fire crackling on the hearth in front of them. She traced a gentle finger down his lean jaw as she said softly, "Then the food—the champagne—it's for us?"

"That's right." He nodded toward a record player in the corner. "Even soft music to help my cause."

"Something like Debussy's 'Sunken Cathedral' or 'Row, Row, Row Your Boat'?"

"How about 'Rocked in the Cradle of the Deep'?" He felt her sudden shiver and pulled her abruptly to her feet. "You're still cold. That coffee water must be ready by now."

She pulled him back as he would have gone toward the kitchen. "I don't want any coffee."

"Something to eat." Amusement vied with something else in his glance.

"I'm not hungry." She moved back a step. "Now don't start giving orders again."

"All I ever said," he reminded her mildly, "was for you to take your wet clothes off and then get to bed."

"I *did* change clothes." She nodded toward the couch. "It's not my fault if the bed isn't ready."

The barest vestige of a smile passed over his face. "That's where you're wrong. It's been ready for days." He nodded calmly toward the stairs. "Your bed's up there."

Jean trembled as she felt the warmth of his hands through the thin silk at her shoulders. Slowly, deliberately he pulled her closer. As those strong hands moved caressingly down, hers went up around his neck.

Untended, the belt at her waist simply gave up the struggle.

It was much, much later that night when Jean felt she should make one thing clear.

"I hope," she said, pushing up on an elbow and addressing Grant's prone form on the bed beside her, "that you don't think I slipped on purpose when I came down that rock this afternoon."

He sighed comfortably and pulled her back down by his side, bestowing a husbandly kiss on her ear in the process. "You stick to your story, darling."

"But I didn't plan it that way," she insisted.

"Who cares?" He yawned profoundly and thumped the pillow to accommodate them both. "If you hadn't

174

slipped, I would have tripped you . . . so it's just as well. Imagine manhandling your wife."

"Manhandling—is that what you call it," she said in pleased discovery. Her eyes crinkled with amusement. "Well, it took you long enough to start the project, my dear. Don't ever abandon your research."

Her soft laugh was stifled as he promptly accepted the challenge and his mouth came purposefully down on hers.

"You should know by now," he assured her eventually, "that I don't intend to."